"Do you live here all the time?" she asked, her voice hushed.

"Not as a rule. Usually I'm here on the weekends only. It's where I come to unwind."

A shiver passed over her. "So I'll be on my own after today?"

"No, Maeve. Until you feel more at home, I'll stay with you."

"In the same room and the same...bed?"

Is that what you'd like? he wanted to ask, beset by memories he almost wished he could forget. Once upon a time they had shared such insatiable passion for each other. "You have your own room for as long as you want it. But I'll never be far away if you need me," he said.

Some people know practically from birth that they're going to be writers. CATHERINE SPENCER wasn't one of them. Her first idea was to be a nun, which was clearly never going to work! A series of other choices followed. She considered becoming a veterinarian (lacked the emotional stamina to deal with sick and injured animals), a hairdresser (until she overheated a curling iron and singed about five inches of hair off the top of her best friend's head, the day before her first date), or a nurse (but that meant emptying bedpans. Eee-yew!) As a last resort, she became a high school English teacher, and loved it.

Eventually she married, had four children and always, always a dog or two or three. How can a house become a home without a dog? she asks. How does an inexperienced mother cope with babies, if she doesn't have a German shepherd nanny?

In time, the children grew up and moved out on their own—as children are wont to do, regardless of their mother's pleading that they remain babies who don't mind being kissed in public! She returned to teaching, but a middle-aged restlessness overtook her and she looked for a change of career.

What's an English teacher's area of expertise? Well, novels, among other things, and moody, brooding, unforgettable heroes—Heathcliff...Edward Fairfax Rochester...Romeo...Rhett Butler. Then there's that picky business of knowing how to punctuate and spell, what "rules" of sentence structure are, and how to break them for dramatic effect. They all pointed her in the same direction: breaking the rules every chance she got, and creating her own moody, brooding unforgettable heroes. And where do they belong? In Harlequin Presents®, of course, which is where she happily resides now.

THE COSTANZO BABY SECRET
CATHERINE SPENCER

~ CLAIMING HIS LOVE-CHILD ~

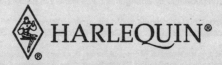

HARLEQUIN®

TORONTO • NEW YORK • LONDON
AMSTERDAM • PARIS • SYDNEY • HAMBURG
STOCKHOLM • ATHENS • TOKYO • MILAN • MADRID
PRAGUE • WARSAW • BUDAPEST • AUCKLAND

Recycling programs
for this product may
not exist in your area.

ISBN-13: 978-0-373-52765-6

THE COSTANZO BABY SECRET

First North American Publication 2010.

THE COSTANZO
BABY SECRET

CHAPTER ONE

At ten o'clock on the morning of September 4, exactly one month to the day since the accident, Dario Costanzo received a phone call he'd begun to fear would never arrive.

"I have news, *signor*," Arturo Peruzzi, chief neurologist in charge of Maeve's case, announced. "This morning, your wife awoke from her coma."

Sensing from the man's neutral tone that there was more to come that didn't bode well, Dario steeled himself to hear the rest. Over the last several weeks, he'd conducted enough research to know that brain damage resulting from a head injury came in many shapes and sizes, none of them good. "But? There is a 'but,' is there not, Doctor?"

"That is correct."

He'd thought himself prepared and found he wasn't prepared at all. Images of her as she'd looked the last time he'd seen her, with her head swathed in bandages and the rest of her hooked up to a bewildering array of tubes to keep her alive, clashed horribly with the way she'd been before everything began to go wrong.

Lovely, graceful, elegant.

Sunlight in motion.

His.

And now? Abruptly, he sat down at his desk, afraid his legs would give way beneath him. "Tell me," he said.

"Physically she shows every sign of making a full recovery. Naturally she's very weak at present, but with appropriate therapy, we anticipate she'll soon be well enough to continue her convalescence at home. The problem, Signor Costanzo, is her mind."

Ah, *Dio*, not that! Better she had died than—

"…not to alarm you unduly. This is quite common following the kind of trauma she sustained, and is by no means as serious as you might suppose."

Realizing that in leaping to the worst possible conclusion, he'd missed what appeared to be a more optimistic prognosis, Dario wrenched his attention back to the neurologist's measured tones. "Exactly what are you suggesting, Doctor?"

"I'm suggesting nothing, *signor*. I'm telling you bluntly that your wife is suffering from retrograde amnesia. In short, she has no memory of her…recent past."

Peruzzi's hesitation was brief, but telling enough to arouse Dario's worst fears all over again. "How recent?"

"That's what makes her case unusual. As a rule, retrograde amnesia applies only to events immediately prior to the injury. In this instance, however, your wife's memory loss extends over a longer period. I am sorry to say that she does not appear to remember you or the life you shared."

Psychogenic amnesia…hysterical amnesia…. Terms that had meant little or nothing to him a month ago, but with which he'd become all too familiar since, floated to the forefront of Dario's mind. "Are you saying her amnesia is psychologically induced, as opposed to physiologically?"

"It would appear so. But the good news is that, regardless of which label we apply, the condition is rarely permanent. In time she will almost certainly regain her memory."

"How much time?"

"That I cannot predict. No one can. It's possible that she could recall everything within minutes of her returning to familiar territory. More likely, it will take days or even weeks, with flashes of memory trickling back in random order. What you must understand is that nothing is to be gained by trying to force her to remember that which, for whatever reason, she cannot recollect. Doing so could be highly detrimental to her well-being. And that, Signor Costanzo, brings me to the crux of this conversation. We have done our part. Now you must do yours."

"How?"

How—the word had hounded him for over a month, begging for answers no one could give. How had he so badly misjudged the depth of her discontent? How, after all they'd promised each other, could she have turned to another man? How had she shown so little faith in *him,* her husband?

"Patience is the key. Bring her home when she's ready to leave the clinic, but don't immediately expose her to a crowd of strangers. Begin by making her feel safe and secure with you."

"How do I do that if she doesn't even remember me?"

"Once she is a little stronger, we'll explain to her who you are. We have no choice. You're her only next of kin, and she needs to know she is not alone in this world. But she has lost a year of her life, a frightening thing for anyone to face. Let her see that you care about the person she remembers herself to be. Then, as her trust in you grows, slowly reintroduce her to the rest of your family."

"The rest of my family happens to include our seven-month-old son. What do you suggest I do with him in the meantime? Pass him off as belonging to the cook?"

If the good doctor picked up on his sarcasm, he gave no sign. "Hide him," he said bluntly. "You have a sister and parents living close by. Surely one of them will look after him for a while?"

"Deceive her, you mean? How is that helping her?"

"The burden of guilt associated with her learning she has an infant son whom she's wiped from her memory might well shatter her sense of worth and leave her with permanent emotional scars. It goes against the very nature of motherhood for any normal woman to forget she bore a child. Of everything that has made up the fabric of your wife's life over the last year, *this* is the most delicate, and how you handle it, definitely the most critical."

"I see." And he did. Maeve might have woken up from her coma, but she was far from healed. "Is there anything else?"

"Yes. For now, do not expect her to be more than a wife in name only. Intimacy and what it connotes, with a man who might be her husband, but is, in fact, a virtual stranger, is a complication she can do without."

Fantastic! The one thing they'd always been good at was no longer in the cards, and he had to farm out Sebastiano to relatives. "Is there anything I *can* do to help her—besides sleep in another room and send our son to live somewhere else?"

"Certainly there is," Peruzzi informed him. "Your wife has lost her memory, not her intellect. She will have questions.

Answer them truthfully, but only as much as she asks for. In other words, don't elaborate, and above all don't try to rush matters. Think of each small fact you reveal as a building block in the empty canvas of her memory. When enough blocks are in place, she'll begin filling in the rest by herself."

"And if she doesn't like everything she learns?"

"It then becomes imperative that you, *signor,* remain calm and supportive. She must know that she can rely on you, regardless of what has happened in the past. Can you do that?"

"Yes," he said dully. What other choice did he have? "May I visit her in the meantime?"

"I cannot forbid it, but I urge against it. Regaining her physical stamina is enough for her to deal with at present, and your inserting yourself into the picture is more likely to compromise her progress than help it. Let it be enough that you'll soon be together again, with the rest of your lives to reestablish your connection to each other."

"I understand," Dario said, even though it was so far from the truth as to be laughable. "And I appreciate your taking time from your busy schedule to speak with me."

"It has been my pleasure. Would that I had such encouraging news to offer the families of all my patients. I will be in touch again when your wife is ready to come home. Meanwhile, I and her other doctors are always available to discuss her progress and address any concerns you might have. *Ciao,* Signor Costanzo, and good luck."

"Grazie e ciao."

Returning the phone to its cradle, Dario paced moodily to the window. In the shelter of the walled garden directly outside his study, Marietta Pavia, the young nanny he'd hired, sat on a blanket, singing to her charge. That a wife could forget the husband she'd grown tired of was understandable, if far from flattering. But how was it possible, he wondered bleakly, that a mother could erase from her mind and heart all memory of her firstborn?

Behind him another voice, cultured, authoritative, interrupted his musings. "I overheard enough to gather there's been a change in her condition."

Swinging around, he confronted his visitor. Black hair smoothed in a perfect classic chignon, and immaculately turned out in a slim-fitting ecru linen dress relieved only by the baroque pearls at her throat and ears, Celeste Costanzo belied her fifty-nine years and could easily have passed for a well-preserved forty-five. "You look ready to take the Milan fashion world by storm, Mother, rather than relaxing on the island," he remarked.

"Just because one is out of the public eye on Pantelleria is no reason to be slovenly, Dario—and don't change the subject. What is the latest news?"

"Maeve has emerged from her coma and is expected to make a full recovery."

"Then she's going to live?"

"Try not to sound so disappointed," he said drily. "She is, after all, the mother of your only grandson."

"She is an unmitigated disaster and I fail to understand why, in light of everything that happened, you continue to defend her."

"But that's the whole point, Mother. We can only guess at what really happened. Of the two people who know for sure, one is dead and the other has lost her memory."

"So that's her game now, is it? Pretending she can't remember she was leaving you and taking your son with her?" His mother curled her lip scornfully. "How convenient!"

"That's preposterous and you know it. Maeve's in no shape to put on any sort of act, and even if she were, her doctors are too experienced to be taken in by it."

"So you buy their diagnosis?"

"I do, and so must you."

"I'm afraid not, my son."

"I advise you to rethink that decision if you wish to be made welcome in my home," he suggested coldly.

Celeste's smooth olive complexion paled. "I am your mother!"

"And Maeve is still my wife."

"For how long? Until she decides to run away again? Until you find Sebastiano living on the other side of the world and calling some other man *Papa?* Tell me what it will take, Dario, to make you see her for the kind of woman she is."

"She's the woman who bore my son," he ground out, the anger that had festered for weeks threatening to boil over. "For all our sakes, kindly refrain from pointing out what you deem to be her shortcomings as a parent or a wife."

Unmoved, his mother said, "I don't imagine I'll have to, my dear. She'll do so for me."

Everyone at the clinic, from the lowliest aide to the loftiest doctor, who'd been so kind to her and looked after her so well came to say goodbye.

And who, when she'd asked what had happened to her, had said only that she'd been in a car accident and shouldn't worry that she couldn't remember because, eventually, it would all come back.

And who'd steadfastly waved aside her concerns about who was sending her flowers and paying the bills—all except for one young aide who'd carelessly let slip that "he" was, before the charge nurse shushed him with a glare that would have turned the Sahara to solid ice.

He who? Maeve wanted to demand, but sensing that answer wouldn't be forthcoming, instead asked, "Am I at least allowed to know where I'm going when I leave here?"

"Of course," the nurse said, adopting the sort of soothing tone one might apply to a fractious child. "Back to the place where you lived before, with the people who love you."

Wherever that was!

A few days before she was discharged, the doctors told her she was going to convalesce in a place called Pantelleria. She'd never heard of it.

"Who'll be there?" she asked.

"Dario Costanzo…"

She'd never heard of him, either.

"…your husband," they said.

And that left her too speechless to persist with any more questions.

Gathered now around the black limousine waiting to take her away, they all showered her with good wishes. "We'll miss you," they chorused, smiling and waving. "Stop in and see us when you're in the neighborhood, but under your own steam the next time."

And suddenly, after days of wanting nothing more than to be free of their round-the-clock vigilance, she was afraid to leave them. They were "after the accident" and all that anchored her to the present. "Before" was a missing chapter in the book of her life. That she was about to rediscover it and the man she'd apparently married during that time, should have filled her with elation. Instead it left her terrified.

Sensing her panic, the young nurse accompanying her to the airport touched her arm sympathetically. "Don't be alarmed," she said. "I'll see you safely to the plane."

The thought of mingling with the general public appalled her. She'd seen herself in a mirror and knew what a spectacle she presented. Despite the clinic's excellent food and the hours she'd lately spent in the sunlit gardens, she remained gaunt and pale. Her hair, once long and thick, was short now, no more than four or five inches, and barely covered the long curving scar above her left ear. Her clothes hung on her as if she'd lost a ton of weight or was suffering from some unspeakable illness.

When the car she was in arrived at the airport, though, it drew up not outside the departure terminal, but took a side road to a tarmac quite separate from the main runways, where a private jet stood and a uniformed steward waited to usher her aboard.

What kind of man was her husband, that she was entitled to such luxury, she who'd grown up in a working-class neighborhood in east Vancouver, the only child of a plumber and a supermarket cashier?

Remembering her parents and how much they'd loved the daughter born to them years after they'd given up hope of ever having children brought a rush of tears to her eyes. If they were still alive, she'd be going home to them, to the safe, neat little rancher on the maple-shaded street, half a block from the park where she'd learned to ride a two-wheeler bike when she was seven.

Her mom would fuss over her and bake her a blackberry pie, and her dad would tell her again how proud of her he was that she'd made something of herself and become such a success. But they were both dead, her father within weeks of retiring at sixty-eight, her mother three years later, and the neat little rancher sold to strangers. As a result, Maeve, already exhausted by the emotional upheaval of the day, was strapped in a divinely comfortable leather seat in an obscenely luxurious private aircraft, headed for a life that was nothing but a big, mysterious question mark.

CHAPTER TWO

ALTHOUGH not exactly chatty, when Mauve asked more about the place she was being taken to, the flight attendant wasn't quite as tight-lipped as the medical personnel had been.

"It is called Pantelleria," he said in careful English, as he served her a late lunch of poached chicken breast and asparagus spears so tender and young, they were almost premature.

"So I understand. But I don't think I'm familiar with it."

"It is an island, known also as the black pearl of the Mediterranean."

"And still part of Italy?"

"*Sì, signora.* Close to one hundred kilometers south-west of the extreme tip of Sicily and less than eighty from Tunisia, which is in Africa."

She hadn't lost all her marbles. She knew where Africa was, *and* Tunisia, but Pantelleria? The name still didn't ring a bell. "Tell me about this black pearl."

"It is small, windy and isolated, and the road circling the island is not good, but the grapes are sweet, the sea is a clear, beautiful blue, the snorkeling and the sunsets *magnifico.*"

It sounded like a paradise. Or a prison. "Do many people live there?"

"Except for the tourists, not so many."

"Have I lived there very long?"

She'd veered too far from the geographical to the personal. His face closed, and he straightened his posture as if he were on a parade ground and about to undergo military inspection. "May I offer you something to drink, *signora*?" he inquired woodenly.

She smiled, hoping to trick him into another revelation. "What do I usually have?"

The effort was wasted. His guard was up. "We have wine, juice, milk and *acqua minerale frizzante* on board or, if you wish, I can serve you espresso."

"Sparkling mineral water," she said testily, and decided that whoever met her when she arrived had better be prepared to give her some straightforward answers, because this whole secrecy conspiracy was getting old very fast.

But the questions bursting to be asked fled her mind when the aircraft skimmed in for landing and, descending the steps to the tarmac, she saw the man waiting to greet her.

If Pantelleria was the black pearl of the Mediterranean, he was its imperial topaz prince. Well over six feet tall, broad, sun-bronzed and so handsome she had to avert her gaze lest she inadvertently started drooling, he took her hand and said, "*Ciao*, Maeve. I'm your husband. It's good to have you home again and see you looking so well."

His thick black hair was expertly barbered, his jaw clean shaven. He had on tan linen trousers and a light blue shirt she recognized was made of Egyptian cotton, and sported a Bulgari watch on his wrist. By comparison, she looked like something the cat dragged in, and ludicrously out of place juxtaposed next to this well-dressed stranger and presumable owner the sleek private jet.

Privately he must have thought so, too, because, despite his kind words, when she ventured another glance at him, she saw the same pity in his dark gray eyes that had dogged her throughout her teenage years.

Desperate to give her advantages neither of them had enjoyed, her parents had almost bankrupted themselves to send her to one of the best private high schools in the city, never realizing the misery their sacrifice had caused her. They'd hidden their words behind their hands, those snooty fellow students born to old money and pedigrees, but she'd heard them anyway, and they had left scars worse than anything a car accident could inflict.

Poor thing, she could eat corn through a picket fence with those teeth....

No wonder she hides behind all that hair....

I feel bad not inviting her to my party, but she just doesn't fit in....

An orthodontist had eventually given her a perfect smile, and flashing it now to hide the crippling shyness that still struck when she felt at a disadvantage, she said, "You'll have to forgive me. I'm afraid your name's slipped my mind."

They had to be the most absurd words ever to fall out of her mouth, but if he thought so, too, he managed to hide it and said simply, "It's Dario."

"Dario." She tried out the word, splitting it into three distinct syllables as he had and copying his intonation, as if doing so would somehow make it taste familiar on her tongue.

It didn't. She paused, hoping he'd enlarge on their relationship with a few pertinent details, and caught something else in his eyes. Disappointment? Reproach?

Whatever it was, he masked it quickly and gestured at the vehicle parked a few yards away. Not a long black limousine this time, but a metallic-gray Porsche Cayenne Turbo, which, although much smaller, she knew came with a hefty price tag attached. "Let's get in the car," he said. "The wind is like a blast furnace this afternoon."

Indeed, yes. Her hair, or what remained of it, stood up like wheat stalks, and perspiration trickled between her breasts. She was glad to slide into the front passenger seat and relax in the cooling draft from the air conditioner; glad that she was on the last leg of the journey to wherever. Though the flight had lasted no more than a couple of hours from takeoff to landing, fearful anticipation of what lay ahead had left her weary to the bone.

Since Dario was so clearly disinclined to talk, she turned her attention to the passing scene as he drove away from the little airport, praying something she saw might trigger a memory, however slight. Soon they were headed south along the coast road the flight attendant had mentioned. It was narrow and winding, but picturesque enough.

To the left, neat patchwork vineyards protected by stone walls rose up the hillsides. Groves of stunted olive trees hugged the earth as if only by doing so could they prevent the winds from sweeping them out to sea.

On the right, turquoise waves shot through with emerald surged over slabs of lava rock rising black along the jagged shoreline. Hence the island's other name, no doubt.

At one point they passed through a charming fishing village. Odd, cube-shaped houses were clustered next to each other with perforated domes or channels on their flat roofs.

"To catch the rainwater," Dario explained, when curiosity got the better of her enough that she dared break his rather forbidding silence and ask what they were for. "Pantelleria is a volcanic island with many underground springs, but the sulphur content makes the water undrinkable."

Disappointingly, this meager tidbit of information struck no more of a chord than anything else she saw. Which left quizzing her laconic husband her only other option if she wanted to arrive at her destination with at least some point of reference in a life dismayingly bereft of landmarks.

"Your flight attendant told me this island's quite small," she said, as the minutes ticked by and he made no further effort to engage her in conversation.

"*Sì.*"

"So your house isn't very far away?"

"Nothing's very far away. Pantelleria is only fourteen and a half kilometers long and less than five kilometers wide."

"So we'll arrive soon?"

"*Sì.*"

"I understand that's where we lived before the accident."

A muscle twitched in his jaw. "*Sì.*"

Talk about a man of few words! "And we've been married how long?"

"A little more than a year."

"Are we happy?"

He tensed visibly, a scowl marring his forehead. "Apparently not."

Distressed, she stared at him. She had exchanged vows with this gorgeous man. Taken his name and presumably once worn his ring, although there was no sign of it now. Had slept in his arms, awakened to his kisses. And somehow let it all slip away.

"Why not?"

He shrugged and gripped the steering wheel more tightly. He had beautiful hands. Long-fingered and elegant. And there was no sign of a wedding ring. "Our living arrangement was not ideal."

She ached to ask him what he meant by that, but the reserve in his voice was hard to miss even for someone in her impaired mental state, so she once again focused her attention on her surroundings.

He'd turned the car off the main road and was navigating a private lane leading to an enclave of secluded villas perched on a headland. By some high-tech method she couldn't begin to fathom, a pair of iron gates set in a high rock wall opened as he approached, then swung smoothly closed again immediately afer the car had passed through.

A drive bordered with dwarf palm trees wound through extensive grounds to a residence which, while remaining true to what appeared to be a traditional island dwelling, was much larger than any they'd passed on the way, and bore an air of unmistakable opulence. Single-storied, it sprawled over the land in a series of terraced cubes, with a domed roof over the larger, central section.

Dario stopped the car outside a massive front door and switched off the ignition. "This is it?" she breathed.

"This is it," he said. "Welcome home, Maeve."

She opened her door and stepped out. The wind had

dropped and a stand of pine trees dusted with the mauve shadows of dusk filled the air with their scent. The first stars blinked in the sky. Even from this vantage point, the estate—and *estate* was the only word to describe it—commanded a magnificent view across the Mediterranean.

Closing her eyes, she breathed in the peace and wondered how she could not remember such a place.

For a moment he leaned against the car and watched. The sight of her body, silhouetted sharp and brittle against the deepening twilight, brought back the shock he'd experienced when she first stepped out of the aircraft. The very second he saw her, he'd wanted to establish his husbandly right to enfold her in his arms. Peruzzi's warning not to crowd her had been all that stopped him. That, and his fear that he might inadvertently break her ribs.

She had always been slender, but never to the point that the siroccos of autumn might blow her away if she ventured too close to the edge of the cliffs. Never to the point of such fragility that she was almost transparent. Small wonder the good doctor had urged him to patience. Restoring her physical stamina had to come first. The rest—their history, the accident and the events leading up to it—could wait. Ambushed by her intuitive questions, he'd already revealed more than he intended, but he wouldn't make the same mistake again. He hadn't risen to the top of a world-wide multi-billion-dollar business empire without learning to dissemble if the occasion called for it. And from where he stood, this amounted to one of those occasions.

"Would you like to stay out here for a while?" he asked her. "Perhaps stretch your legs with a stroll through the gardens?"

She ran her fingers through her short, silky hair. "No, thank you. Even though it's still early, I find I'm quite tired."

"Come then, and I'll have my housekeeper show you to your room."

"Do I know her?"

"No. She started working for me just last week. Her predecessor moved to Palermo to be closer to her grandchildren."

He took her one small suitcase from the back of the car and pushed open the front door, then stood back to let her precede him inside the house.

She stepped into the wide foyer and slowly inspected her surroundings, taking in the lazy motion of the fans suspended from the high ceiling, the cool white walls, the black marble floors. "Do you live here all the time?" she asked, her voice hushed.

"Not as a rule. Usually I'm here on the weekends only. It's where I come to unwind."

A shiver passed over her. "So I'll be on my own after today?"

"No, Maeve. Until you feel more at home, I'll stay with you."

"In the same room and the same…bed?"

Is that what you'd like? he wanted to ask, beset by memories he almost wished he could forget. Once upon a time, they had shared such insatiable passion for each other. "You have your own room for as long as you want it, but I'll never be far away if you need me," he said instead, and congratulated himself on providing an answer that neither threatened her, nor shut the door on their resuming a more normal married life at some future point. Peruzzi would be proud of him.

"Oh," she said, and he might almost have thought she sounded disappointed. "Well, that's very nice and considerate of you. Thank you."

"Prego."

She inched a little closer. "Um…are my clothes and personal effects still here?"

"Yes," he assured her. "Everything is exactly as you left it." Except for the blood-soaked outfit she wore the day of the accident. That was one memory he wished he could erase and hoped she'd never recall. "Here's Antonia now," he continued, relieved to be able to change the subject as the housekeeper arrived on the scene. "She'll take you to your suite and make sure you have everything you need."

She exchanged a tentative smile with Antonia, then turned to him one last time. "Thank you again for everything you've done today."

"It was nothing," he said. "Sleep well and I'll see you in the morning."

As soon as the two women, one so sturdy, the other so frail, left the entrance hall and disappeared toward the lower left wing of the house where the guest bedrooms were located, he turned in the opposite direction and along the corridor that led to the library and his home office. Closing himself in the latter, he picked up the phone and called Giuliana, his sister, who lived next door.

"I was hoping I'd hear from you," she said, picking up on the first ring. "Did Maeve arrive home safely?"

"She did."

"And how is she? Is it as bad as we feared?"

"Ah, Giuliana!" Horrified, he heard his voice crack and had to take a moment to collect himself. "She's fragile as spun glass, inside and out. The journey down here exhausted her. We got in just a few minutes ago and she went straight to bed."

"Poor thing! I wish I could see her and tell her how much I love her and how glad I am to have her back among us."

"I wish it, too. I wish you could bring her son home and have her look at him and recognize at once that she's his mother. Sadly, the time's not yet right."

"I know, Dario. Small steps, isn't that what her doctor said?"

"Yes, but not, I fear, as small as he'd like. Already she's wormed too much information out of me and knows our marriage was on shaky ground. Not exactly the best way for us to start trying to put our lives back together, is it?"

"But it can be done if you love each other enough to fight for what you once had. The question is, do you?"

"I can't speak for her, Giuliana."

"Then speak for yourself. I know that the way you started out together wasn't ideal, and that you married her because you believed it was the honorable thing to do and you had no other choice, but it seemed to me that you were making it work."

"Until it all went horribly wrong."

And therein lay the crux of the matter. Could either of them get past what had happened, or had they lost too much ground ever to trust each other again?

Seeming to read his thoughts, his sister said softly, "Maeve loves you, Dario. I am certain of that."

"Are you?" he said wearily. "I wish I was. But I didn't call to burden you with my doubts, I called to find out how you're holding up having an extra child to care for. Is Sebastiano wearing you out?"

"Not in the least. Marietta is an enormous help. You were

lucky to find so capable and willing a nanny. As for Cristina, she loves her little cousin and plays with him all the time. And he's such a contented baby. He only ever cries if he's hungry or tired, or needs to be changed."

"He's the one bright spot in this whole unfortunate business."

"And too young to understand what's happened."

"Let's hope he never will." Dario paused. "Has anyone else in the family stopped by to see him?"

"If by that you mean our mother, then, yes. She came by this morning and again this afternoon. She's quite adamant that he should be staying with her, and I'm equally adamant that he should not."

"I'd hoped she'd go back to Milan with our father. The last thing Maeve needs right now is to run afoul of her."

"Unfortunately, she seems set on staying here. But don't worry, Dario. I can hold my own with her, as you very well know, and Lorenzo certainly can. He won't stand for her interfering in our arrangement."

That much he knew to be true. His mother might be a handful at times, but his brother-in-law was no more a man to be pushed around than Dario himself was. "I'm grateful to both of you for your support. Kiss my son good-night for me, will you? I'd come over and do it myself, but—"

"No," his sister cut in. "Tonight, at least, it's more important that you stay home in case Maeve needs you. It wouldn't do for her to find herself alone before she gets her bearings."

And how long before that happened, he wondered moodily, ending the call and pouring himself a stiff drink. It was all very fine for Arturo Peruzzi to counsel patience, but Dario had never been a particularly patient man. Already, after little more than an hour, his tolerance was tested to the limit as far as letting nature take its course in its own sweet time. He'd spent too many days neglecting work because he couldn't concentrate. Too many evenings like this, with a bottle of single-malt Scotch for company. And a damn sight too many nights alone in a bed designed for two.

Irritably, he threw open the glass doors and stepped out onto the terrace. Night had fallen and the dozens of solar lights dotted throughout the garden and around the perimeter of the pool gleamed softly in the dark.

Once upon a time not so very long ago, Maeve had wanted him as much as he wanted her. They'd slipped naked into the warm, limpid depths of the private spa outside their bedroom and made love with an urgency that bordered on desperation. He'd buried his mouth against hers for fear that someone might hear her cries of surrender. He'd withheld his own pleasure in order to prolong hers, and finally come so hard and fast within the confines of her sleek, tight flesh that his heart almost stopped.

So why was he standing here alone now, hard and aching, and she was sleeping in a guest suite? *Dannazione,* she was his wife!

A sound punctured the night, closer than the murmur of the restless sea, fainter than a whisper. A footfall so hesitant he might have dismissed it as a figment of his imagination had it not been accompanied by a fragrance he recognized: bergamot, juniper and Sicilian mandarin softened with a touch of rosemary. *Her* fragrance, and he ought to know. He'd bought it for her.

Turning his head, he found her framed in the open doorway behind him, her silhouette softened this time by the long, loose garment she'd put on. She had never looked more ethereal or desirable.

"I thought you'd turned in for the night," he said when he was able to speak.

"I couldn't sleep."

"Too much excitement?"

"Perhaps." She took a step toward him and then another. "Or perhaps I've done enough sleeping and it's time for me to wake up."

CHAPTER THREE

HE REMAINED so still and watched her so warily that she almost lost her nerve and scuttled back to the safety of her suite. Decorated in shades of celadon and cream, nice soothing colors designed not to agitate the amnesiac mistress of the house, it was more luxurious than anything she could have imagined. The gorgeous bathroom had a steam shower and a tub deep enough to drown in. Adjacent to the bedroom was a sitting room, and outside in the private garden overlooking the sea, a swimming pool.

An oasis of tranquility, she'd have thought, yet she'd found neither answers nor rest there. From the minute she stepped over the threshold into the house, an air of utter desolation had engulfed her. She felt hollow inside. Bereft beyond anything words could describe.

Something bad had happened here. Something that went beyond a less than perfect marriage, and try though she might to dismiss it, the weight of unspeakable tragedy, of an event or events too horrific to contemplate, continued to haunt her. This spectacular seaside villa held a dark and dreadful secret, one she was determined to unearth. And whether or not he wanted to, her tight-lipped husband was the man who'd reveal it to her.

"Are you going to offer me a drink?" she asked boldly, even though her pulse ran so fast that she could hardly breathe. Nothing new there, though. She'd lived with subdued panic most of her life, and had long ago learned to disguise it behind a facade of manufactured poise.

"If you're asking for alcohol, I'm not sure that I should," Dario said.

"Why not? Am I a raging dipsomaniac?"

He actually laughed at that, a lovely rich ripple of sound that played over her nerve endings like the bass keys of a finely tuned piano. "Hardly."

"That's a relief. For a moment, I was afraid I might be a good-time girl who danced on the table after one beer."

"I've never known you to drink beer. You prefer good champagne, and never more than a glass or two at that. Nor have I ever seen you dance on a table."

"Then why the reluctance to humor me now?"

"Medication and alcohol aren't a good mix."

"I'm not taking any medication. Haven't for more than two weeks."

"I see," he said and ran a hand over his jaw. "In that case, I'll make you a deal. Join me for dinner and I'll crack open a bottle of your favorite vintage. It was always your favorite."

Not wanting to appear too eager, she pretended to give the matter some thought. "All right. Now that you mention it, I am rather hungry."

"*Eccellente*. If you'll excuse me for a moment, I'll let the cook know there'll be two of us dining tonight."

"Of course." She waited until he'd disappeared then, weak at the knees from his departing smile, she tottered to a pair of sun lounges upholstered in blue-and-white-striped cotton, and practically fell onto the one nearest.

The view spread out in front of her was breathtaking. A big oval infinity pool, strategically placed for maximum dramatic effect, appeared to cling to the very rim of the cliff. An illusion, of course, brought about by the sort of complicated engineering feat only the very rich and famous could afford. But the profusion of bougainvillea framing the picture was nature's handiwork alone.

Dario returned in a matter of minutes with two slender tulip-shaped flutes and a silver ice bucket containing a bottle of champagne. He poured the wine, sat down beside her and touched the rim of his glass to hers. *"Salute!"*

"Salute! And thank you."

"For what?"

"For everything you've done since I've been ill. They told me at the hospital that you're the one who sent me flowers every day and who took care of all my expenses."

"What else would you have had me do, Maeve? I'm your husband."

"Yes, well…about that…"

"Relax, *cara,*" he advised her gently. "I didn't mention our relationship as a prelude to demanding my conjugal rights."

"Oh," she said, swallowing a wave of disappointment along with a sip of champagne. Not that she was raring to make love to a man she didn't know, but that he presumably knew her very well indeed, yet was so willing to keep his distance, wasn't exactly flattering. On the other hand, what else did she expect? "Under the circumstances, it never occurred to me that you were."

He turned his head sharply and fixed her in a probing stare. "What do you mean by that?"

"I might not remember marrying you, Dario, but I've still got twenty-twenty vision. I know I look more like a scarecrow than a woman."

"You're still recovering from an accident that almost cost you your life. You can't expect to look the same as you did before."

"Even so, my hair..." She tugged self-consciously at the pathetic remains of what had once been her crowning glory, as if doing so might persuade it to sprout another few inches.

Reaching across the space separating them, he stilled her hand and brought it down to rest beneath his. It was the kind of thing a parent might do to stop a child picking at a scab, but however he might have intended it, his touch electrified her in places not referred to in polite society. Involuntarily she clamped her knees together as primly as a virgin defending her innocence.

Fortunately, he couldn't read her mind. Or if he could, he didn't like the direction it had taken, because he let go of her hand as quickly as he'd grasped it. "You have beautiful hair," he said. "It reminds me of sunshine on satin."

"It's too short."

"I like it short. It shows more of your face, which, like the rest of you, is also quite beautiful, regardless of how you might view it."

Even though he delivered it as matter-of-factly as a Kennel Club judge might appraise a freshly trimmed poodle, his compliment was more than she'd hoped for or deserved. After her bath, she'd done her best to find something flattering to wear among the clothes she'd discovered in the small dressing room connecting her bedroom to the bathroom, and heaven knew there was quite a bit to choose from.

Layers of lingerie in glass-fronted drawers filled one side, with a shelf of shoes below, and another holding several big floppy sun hats above. Opposite was a row of loose-fitting day dresses, skirts and tops, with two or three more elegant dinner outfits on padded hangers arranged at one end. Nothing too formal, though. Judging by the plethora of beach and patio wear, and the pairs of straw sandals and flip-flops encrusted with crystals, Pantelleria was not the social center of the world.

The quality of the clothes, however, was unmistakable. She'd fingered the expensive fabrics, admiring the cut and color of the various garments. Fashion was in her blood and whatever else might have slipped her mind, her eye for style had not. That most items appeared at least two sizes too large might have proved something of a challenge to a person of lesser experience, but she was on familiar territory when it came to making a woman look her best. Bypassing silky lace-trimmed bras and panties, she'd chosen cotton knit underwear that forgave her diminished curves, and topped it with a loose-flowing caftan in vibrant purple that whispered over her body like a breeze and softened the sharp jut of her hip bones.

Regarding her efforts in the full-length mirror, she'd felt a woman a little more in charge of herself again. But although it had given her the courage to seek out Dario and try to worm more information out of him, now that he was inspecting her so thoroughly, she almost cowered.

"You're embarrassing me," she protested.

"Why?" he countered mildly. "You're lovely, and I can't possibly be the first man to tell you so."

"No. My father used to say the same thing, but he was prejudiced. In truth, I was an ugly duckling, especially as a teenager."

"I quite believe it."

Her jaw dropped. "You do?"

"Certainly. How else could you have turned into such an elegant swan?"

He was laughing at her, and suddenly she was laughing, too.

It had been so long since she'd done that, and the result was startling, as if she'd opened an inner door and set free a hard, dark knot of misery. For the first time in weeks, she felt light and could breathe again. "Thank you for saying that. You're very kind."

"And you're your own worst critic." He touched her again, stroking the back of her hand, his fingers warm and strong. "What happened to make you that way, Maeve?"

"I'd have thought I told you that already, seeing that we're married."

"Perhaps you did," he said, "but since we're starting out all over again, tell me a second time."

"Well, I was always shy, but never more than when I entered my teens. I'd become paralyzed with self-consciousness in a crowd, and had a miserable adolescence as a result."

"Didn't most of us at that age, at one time or another?"

"I suppose, but mine was made worse because, when I turned thirteen, my parents sent me to a very prestigious girls-only private academy, light-years removed from the kind of school I was used to and the few friends I had. Not that I came from the wrong side of the tracks or anything, but the day I walked into that elite establishment sitting across town on its high-priced five acres of prime real estate, I entered a different world, one in which I was a definite outsider."

"You made no new friends?"

"Not really. Teenage girls can be very cruel, even if they don't always mean to be. At best I was tolerated. At worst, ignored. I wasn't entirely blameless, either. I compensated by withdrawing and trying to make myself invisible, which isn't easy when you're taller than everyone else, and painfully awkward to boot. I suppose that's when I became fixated on long hair. I used to hide behind it all the time."

She took another sip of champagne and stared at the empty sea, for the second time in one day harking back to that awful, unhappy era. "I wanted to be different. Be braver, more outgoing, more interesting and lively. More like those other girls who were so sure of themselves and so at ease in their environment. But I was me. Ordinary, dull. Academically acceptable, but socially and athletically inept."

"When did all that change?"

"How do you know it did?"

"Because the person you describe isn't the woman I know."

Not on the outside, perhaps, and usually not on the inside either. Until someone poked too cruelly at those hidden insecurities and made them bleed. Then she was exactly that girl all over again. Not good enough. A nobody masquerading as somebody.

"Maeve," he said, watching her closely, "what happened to make you see yourself in a different light?"

She remembered as if it had occurred just last week. "The day in my senior year that the headmistress called me up on stage during morning assembly and ordered the entire student body to look at Maeve Montgomery and take notice. Believing I was about to be castigated for having broken some unwritten rule of decorum, and to hide the fact that I was shaking inside, I stood very erect and stared out at that sea of faces without blinking."

"And?"

"And what she said was, 'When members of the general public meet girls from this academy walking down the street or waiting at the bus stop, this is what I expect them to see. Someone who doesn't feel the need to raise her voice to draw attention to herself, but who behaves with quiet dignity. Someone proud to wear our uniform, with her blouse tucked in at the waist, her shoes polished and her hair neatly arranged.'"

Maeve paused and shot Dario a wry glance. "In case you're wondering, by then I'd progressed to the point that I wore my hair in a French braid, instead of letting it hang in my face."

"I see. So the girl who thought she was an outsider turned out to fit in very well, after all."

"I suppose I did, in a way. I'm not sure if I was really the paragon of virtue the headmistress made me out to be, or if she understood that I needed a morale boost and that was her way of giving it to me, but after that morning the other seniors regarded me with a sort of surprised respect, and those in the lower grades with something approaching awe."

"What matters, *cara,* is how did you see yourself?"

"Differently," she admitted. That night she'd looked in the

mirror, something she normally avoided, and discovered not a flat-chested, gangly teenager forever tripping over her own feet, but a long-legged stranger with soft curves, straight teeth and clear blue eyes.

Not that she said as much to Dario, of course. She'd have sounded too conceited. Instead she explained, "I realized it was time to get over myself. I vowed I'd never again be ashamed of who I was, but would face the world with courage, and honor the ideals my parents had instilled in me. In other words, to value honesty and loyalty and decency."

"People don't necessarily abide by their promises though, do they?"

Taken aback by the sudden and inexplicably bitter note underlying his remark, she said, "I can't speak for other people, Dario, but I can tell you that I've always tried hard to stick to mine."

He stared her at her for a second or two, his beautiful face so immobile it might have been carved from granite. When he spoke, his voice was as distant as the cold stars littering the sky. "If you say so, my dear. It's such a fine night that I ordered dinner served out here. I hope you don't mind."

"Not at all," she answered, "but I do mind your changing the subject so abruptly."

He turned away with a shrug, as if to say, *And I should care because?* But she was having none of that. She'd been stone-walled long enough by doctors and nurses and therapists. She'd be damned if she'd put up with the same treatment from a man claiming to be her husband.

Grasping his arm, she stopped him before he could put more distance between them. "Don't ignore me, Dario. You implied that I'm lying, and I want to know why. What have I done to make you not believe me?"

Before he could answer, the housekeeper came to announce that dinner was ready. Obviously relieved at the interruption, he took Maeve by the elbow and steered her the length of the terrace, to a table and chairs set under a section of roof that extended from the house. Long white curtains hung to the floor on the open three sides, no doubt to provide protection from the sun and wind during the day, but they were tied back now and gave an unobstructed view of the moon casting a glittering path across the sea.

It was, she thought, as he seated her and took his place opposite, like a scene out of the *Arabian Nights*. Candles glowed in crystal bowls and sent flickering shadows over a marble-topped table dressed with crisp linen napkins and heavy sterling cutlery. Music with a distinctly Middle-Eastern flavor filtered softly from hidden speakers. Some night-blooming flower filled the air with fragrance. Yet the harmony was tainted by the tension still simmering between her and Dario.

Antonia reappeared from inside the house and proceeded to serve from a sideboard positioned next to the wall. The meal began with a salad of tomatoes, olives, onions and capers dressed in oil flavored with basil, followed by grilled swordfish on a bed of linguine. And since Antonia remained at her post well within earshot as they ate, the opportunity to pursue the cause of Dario's sudden change of mood had to go on hold in favor of inconsequential chitchat.

At length, however, the meal was over, the dishes removed and they were alone again. Pushing aside her water goblet, Maeve interrupted him as he waxed eloquent about the therapeutic benefits of the many hot springs on the island, and said, "Okay, Dario, it's just you and me now, so please forget being a tour guide and answer the question I put to you before your housekeeper interrupted us. And don't even think about telling me to forget it, because I've had about as much as I can stand of people not being straight with me."

"I spoke out of turn," he said carefully, seeming to find the contents of his wineglass more riveting than her face. "I've met more than a few business acquaintances whose idea of a gentleman's agreement turned out to be as meaningless as their handshake. Sad to say, it's left me somewhat jaded as a result."

"That's a shame."

"Yes, it is," he agreed, finally meeting her gaze. "I apologize if I insulted you, Maeve. It was not my intention, and I quite understand if you feel compelled to kick me under the table for being such a brute."

His smile was back, dazzling as ever. Basking in its warmth, she said, "I'll forgive you on one condition. So far tonight I've done most of the talking, when what I'd really like is to learn more about you."

"All right."

"And I wouldn't mind going for a walk while I quiz you."

"Are you sure you're up to it? This is your first day out of hospital, after all."

"But I haven't been bedridden for a few weeks now. As long as I don't have to rappel down a cliff or run a marathon, I'm quite sure I'll be fine."

"Then we'll take a stroll through the grounds."

He led her along a crushed stone path that meandered

around to the landward side of the villa and through a series of small gardens.

"Why is each one enclosed like this?" she wanted to know, finding the high stone walls almost claustrophobic.

"To protect them from the winds. These lemon trees here, for instance, would never survive if they were exposed to the sirocco."

She supposed she once knew that, along with the thousand other trivial details that made up daily life on this tiny island, but rediscovering them could wait. For now, sketching in the major figures that shaped her particular situation had to take precedence. "I can see I have a lot to relearn, so let's get started."

"*D'accordo.* Where shall I begin?"

"With your family, since they're also now my family by marriage. Do they live here some of the time, as well?"

"Yes."

"Are they here now?"

"Yes."

"I haven't seen any sign of them."

"They don't actually live in my *dammuso.*"

"You're *what?*"

"*Dammuso,*" he repeated, his grin gleaming in the dark. "Plural, *dammusi.* It's an Arabic word loosely translated as *house* although more accurately meaning *vaulted structure.* The style and method of construction is the same for all residences on Pantelleria."

Not quite, she thought. They might all be shaped like sugar cubes with arched openings and domed roofs, but most were a far cry from the elegant luxury that defined his and the others perched on this remote headland. "Then where *do* they live?"

"Here, we're close neighbors. My sister lives next door, and my parents next door to her."

"And when you're not on the island?"

"Our home base is Milan where our corporate headquarters are located. But we're not on top of each other there the way we are here. In the city, you and I have a penthouse, my parents also, but not in the same building, and my sister and her husband have a villa in the suburbs."

"You have no brothers? Just the one sister?"

"That's right."

"Does she have children?"

"Yes, but it's probably not a good idea to confuse you with too many names and numbers just yet."

"Okay, then tell me about these corporate headquarters, which sound imposingly grand. Exactly what sort of corporation is it?"

"A family business going back over ninety years. Costanzo Industrie del Ricorso Internazionali. You might have heard of it."

She frowned. "I don't think so."

"My great-grandfather started it in the early 1920s. After hearing about and reading of the misery and destruction during World War I, particularly of children left orphaned and homeless, he vowed he'd dedicate himself to creating a better, more beautiful world for those who'd been born into poverty. He began small here in Italy, buying abandoned land and creating parks in areas of our cities where before, rat-infested alleys were the only playgrounds."

"Then you do know of at least one man who kept his word."

"*Sì.*" He acknowledged her gentle dig with another smile. "Eventually, he expanded his idea to include holiday camps in the country for needy children, some of whom had never seen the sea or a lake. To subsidize their operation and make it possible for cash-strapped families to send their sons and daughters away for a few weeks every summer, he turned his entrepreneurial skills in a more lucrative direction, developing ski, golf and beach resorts, at first on his home turf, then in neighboring countries. A portion of the profits went toward setting up endowment funds for his charity work."

"I wish I'd known him. He sounds like a very fine gentleman."

"From all accounts, he was. When he died in the mid-1960s, CIR Internazionali was a household name in Italy. Today, it's recognized worldwide and supports a variety of nonprofit organizations for underprivileged children."

"And where do you fit in the corporate structure?"

"I'm senior vice-president to my father, the chairman and CEO. Specifically, I oversee our European and North American operations."

"So I married an executive giant."

"I suppose you did." By then they'd come to a flight of stone steps that brought them back to the seaward side of the property. "Be careful. These are a little uneven in places," he warned, taking her hand.

This time he didn't release it at the first opportunity, but tucked it more firmly in his. Except for the glow of lamps inside the house and the lights illuminating the infinity pool, the scene was locked in dark blue moon shadows, creating a sense of such isolation that she instinctively tightened her fingers around his. "We might be the only two people left in the world," she murmured.

He caught her other hand and drew her closer. So close that

even though their bodies weren't quite touching, such an electrifying awareness sprang up that she wouldn't have been surprised to see blue sparks arcing between them. "Would it trouble you if, in fact, we were?"

"No," she said, lifting her face to his. "I can think of no one else I'd rather be alone with."

He did then what she'd been wanting him to do from the moment she set eyes on him that afternoon. He lowered his head and kissed her. Not on the cheek, as he had before, but on the mouth. Not coolly, as one person greeting another, but like a man possessed of a hunger he could barely keep in check.

She swayed under the impact. Closed her eyes, dazzled by sudden splendor. Felt his arms go around her and pin her hard against him.

His tongue slid between her lips and she tasted desire. His, hers, theirs, more intoxicating than champagne. And for as long as the kiss lasted, the emptiness that had gripped her from the moment of her arrival at the villa eased just a little.

Then it all slipped away. Lifting his head, he put her at arm's length, his breathing as ragged as hers. "I think you've learned enough for one day," he muttered.

"Not quite," she whispered, the desolation he left behind striking through her heart like a darning needle. "I have one more question begging to be answered."

"What is it?"

"If we can kiss like that, Dario, how is it we weren't happily married?"

CHAPTER FOUR

PERUZZI would not be pleased. "Answer truthfully, but only as much as she asks for," the good doctor had counseled. "Above all, don't try to rush matters."

In theory it had all sounded simple enough. In fact, applying the advice was as dicey as picking a path through a minefield. And kissing her, Dario realized, frustrated on more levels than he cared to number, ranked high on the list of rushing things, at least from his perspective. He was hard and aching and half-blind with hunger for a woman who wouldn't have known him from Adam if she'd happened to pass him on the street. All of which most definitely left him in no shape to field another round of her astute questions.

Playing for time, he said, "What makes you think we weren't happy?"

"You told me so, remember?"

Unfortunately he did, and wished he'd had the good sense to think before he spoke or, failing that, to keep his mouth shut altogether. A chunk of recent history might have gone missing from her memory, but the rest of Maeve's brain was firing on all cylinders.

Despite not being able to see her clearly, the intensity of her gaze burned in the gloom. "Were we on the brink of divorce, Dario?" she persisted.

Were they? Only she knew the answer to that one. "No," he said, sticking strictly to the facts. After all, no papers had been filed, no lawyers called in to divide the marital assets or mediate custodial rights.

"Then what was the problem?"

Racking his brains for a misleadingly truthful reply, he said, "All marriages go through rough patches once in a while."

"But we've been married such a short time," she mourned. "We should have been still on our honeymoon."

Dannazione! Next, she'd be asking where they *spent* their honeymoon, and getting into the circumstances surrounding their wedding would certainly not meet with Peruzzi's approval. "Don't assume, because we might have hit a few bumps along the way, that our marriage was a failure," he temporized. "For every disappointment there were a hundred joys, and for me, having you home again rates as one of the latter."

"If you care that much, why did you never visit me in the hospital?"

Dio dare lui forza! Raising his eyes heavenward, he appealed for help. "I did visit you, Maeve. I sat by your bed day and night for weeks after the accident, praying that you'd live."

"But then you stopped coming. Why?"

Because we have a son who was also hospitalized, and he needed me, too. "For a start, I'd had you transferred to a clinic outside Rome, one renowned for its success in treating brain injuries. But you didn't know I was there, and since I was able to do nothing for you, I focused on what I could do."

"Turned to work to distract you, you mean?"

"Yes," he lied, because he knew the truth would be more than she was ready to hear.

"What about when I woke up from the coma?"

"I would have come to you immediately, but your doctors advised against it. You still had a long way to go before being discharged, and they didn't want anything to interfere with your recovery."

"Since when does seeing her husband impede a woman's recovery?"

"When she doesn't remember him?" he suggested drily.

"Oh." She bit her lip. "Yes, I suppose so."

As much by good luck as good judgment, he'd steered the conversation into safer channels. Before she derailed it with another question he couldn't or shouldn't answer, he said, "Difficult though it might be, you have to slow down, Maeve. When last we spoke, Peruzzi warned me against letting you overdo it. If he were here now, I guarantee he'd be appalled that, after the kind of day you've put in, you're not yet in bed."

"But there's still so much I don't know!"

Ushering her inside the house, he said firmly, "And a hundred tomorrows in which to learn it. At this point, what you need above all else is to get some rest. The last thing either of us wants is for you to suffer a relapse."

He'd found the magic word. "Heavens, no!" she exclaimed with a shudder. "That's the one thing I couldn't face."

"Then I'll say good-night." Keeping a safe distance between them, he bent and brushed his mouth across her cheek. But even so chaste a benediction tempted him beyond bearing. The fabric of her dress whispered over her skin in invitation, reminding him of the smooth, creamy flesh it concealed. And the color, a purple as deep as midnight in the tropics, turned her beautiful eyes an iridescent amethyst.

Clinging to him suddenly, she said on a trembling breath, "I am going to remember us eventually, aren't I?"

"Yes."

"Promise?"

"You have my word." He disentangled himself and shooed her away. "Off you go now. Sleep well, and I'll see you in the morning."

With a last doe-eyed look, she went. Expelling a breath of relief, he strode to the liquor cabinet and poured himself a stiff measure of grappa. The brandy seared his throat, but did nothing to ease the turmoil consuming him.

He hadn't climbed to the top of the corporate ladder through indecision, but through sound judgment and an uncanny ability to read other men. He could sense weakness, detect lack of integrity before an opponent so much as opened his mouth. Yet *she* left him riddled with self-doubt.

Had she surrendered to his kiss because the desire that had run riot in him had taken her hostage, too, or because she saw pandering to his sexual appetite as a way to buy forgiveness for past transgressions? When she'd talked of abiding by her promises and he'd hinted at her duplicity, had her dismay been sincere or a disingenuous cover-up?

He had no answers. Not for her or himself.

That night she dreamed of home. Except it wasn't home any longer. Someone else had moved into her apartment and she stood at her parents' graveside, with all her worldly possessions stacked around her in various crates and traveling trunks. "I'm going away and never coming back," she told her mother and father, "but you'll always be with me in my heart."

The leaves on the trees chattered in a gust of wind. "You can't go. You belong here."

"I must," she protested, indicating a shadowy figure in the distance. "He needs me. I hear him…"

"No." The branches swooped low, binding themselves around her. The leaves piled on top of her, smothering her, holding her captive.

She awoke, tangled in fine cotton sheets, her body bathed in sweat, the blood thundering in her ears. Sunlight flooded the room.

Desperately she tried to hold on to the dream, certain she'd been on the brink of a memory breakthrough. Closing her eyes, she fought to recall the image of that elusive background shape, but the clouds that had inhabited her mind for so long now, closed in again, blotting out the picture. Perhaps tonight or tomorrow…

A knock came at the door. Dario? she wondered.

Full of anticipation, she stumbled out of bed and hurried into the sitting room. "Just a sec," she called, pushing her fingers through her hair in a futile attempt to restore it to some sort of order. Once upon a time, the weight of it would have brought it falling around her shoulders in acceptable disarray. Now it sprang up from her scalp in demented whorls, as if she'd accidentally poked a steel knitting needle into an electrical outlet while she happened to be standing in a tub of water.

Opening the door, she came face-to-face not, as she'd hoped, with her husband, but with Antonia bearing a tray with coffee and a plate of fresh fruit.

Seeming not at all surprised to find Maeve wearing nothing but a short nightgown, the housekeeper nodded amiably and deposited the tray on a table on the terrace. Her English was almost nonexistent, and her Italian laced with a dialect that made it more or less incomprehensible, but, aided by gestures, she managed to convey the fact that the *signor* had eaten breakfast several hours earlier, was not presently at home, but would join the *signora* for lunch at one.

Puzzled, Maeve glanced at the brass clock on a side table, appalled to see that it was after ten already and she'd slept half the morning away. Dismissing the housekeeper, she poured an inch of espresso into a tall narrow latte cup and filled it the rest of the way from a jug of foamy hot milk. She might not remember anything about her previous life in this luxurious hideaway, but she did know she'd never cared for strong black coffee and so, apparently, did the kitchen staff.

The caffeine chased away the lingering remnants of sleep, and left her filled with restless energy. Cradling her latte, she paced the small enclosed garden, stopping occasionally at the table to sample the black grapes, wedges of persimmon and sliced peaches on the fruit plate. Questions dogged her every step. Where had Dario gone? What was the significance of her dream? Why was it haunting her still? What else would she learn today? How long before she remembered everything?

The sun beat down, not the least bit tempered by the steady

wind blowing in from the sea. A smudge of land appearing to float on the horizon must be the coast of north Africa, she surmised. Closer at hand a flowering vine sprawled over the stone wall on her right. To the left another wall, similarly clad, had a solid, tight-fitting gate in its center. Almost at her feet, protected from the wind by a shoulder-high glass screen, the pool shimmered and glimmered in cool invitation.

Well, why not go for a swim? At the very least it might deflect the endless circle of questions parading through her mind. And for that matter, why bother with a bikini since, at her present weight, it'd probably end up around her ankles the minute she hit the water? She was, after all, quite alone. Beyond the glass barrier, the land dropped down some eight feet or more to a terraced garden. The walls on either side were high enough that no one could see over them.

In the lee of the building stood a cart containing, among other things, a stack of folded beach towels. She took one, dropped it on the pool deck, then quickly, before she lost her nerve, she shed her nightgown and dived cleanly into the water.

It felt heavenly; cool satin streaming over her limbs. Surfacing, she swam the length of the pool and back, seven or eight times. Then, breathless from the unaccustomed exercise, she flipped over on her back and floated, loving the freedom, the sense of physical well-being that suffused her body.

Quite when she became aware she was no longer alone, she wasn't certain. It might have been the reflected glint of light on the lens of sunglasses that caught her attention, or the door in the wall standing open where, previously, it had been firmly closed. Or perhaps it was the unpleasant prickle of awareness creeping stealthily up her spine, and the sudden chill in the atmosphere, as if a menacing shadow had passed between her and the sun. But the "how" really didn't matter; what did was that she'd been caught stark naked.

Her reaction was instantaneous. She jack-knifed swiftly under water again and swam to the side of the pool closest to the intruder. Once there, she huddled in the corner, next to the steps, with her knees drawn up to her waist and her arms crossed over her bare breasts.

"It is a little late to be overcome by modesty, my dear," her unwanted visitor declared, lowering her glasses far enough down her patrician nose to inspect her thoroughly. "But then, propriety never has been your forte, has it?"

"I…wasn't expecting company," Maeve stammered, so mortified she wished the bottom would drop out of the pool and sweep her straight into the sea.

"Apparently not."

"I gather we've met before?"

The woman sighed. "Unfortunately, yes."

"I see." And she did. Whatever else this stranger might be, she was no friend. "I'm sorry to say I don't remember you."

"So I've been led to believe." Whoever she was expelled another sigh, more long-suffering than its predecessor. "Would that I were blessed with a similar affliction regarding you. Sadly, that is not so. I remember you all too well."

"And for some reason, don't like me. May I ask why not?"

"You are not one of us. You never will be. Why my son ever spared you a second glance is beyond my understanding."

This woman was her mother-in-law?

The ludicrous indignity of the occasion, with her cowering naked under her adversary's withering scrutiny, revived an old, familiar despair in Maeve. It crept over her like a second skin, cold, clammy and soul destroying. Numbly, she said, "Regardless of what you think of me, will you at least pass me my towel?"

The woman spared her another blistering glare then, with the toe of her elegant shoe, inched the towel within reach. Seizing it, Maeve used it to screen herself until she'd climbed out of the pool, then wound it around her body to cover everything from her breasts to her knees. As a fashion statement, it hardly compared to her mother-in-law's sleek outfit, but it was better than the nothing she'd had on before.

"I regret meeting you again under such embarrassing circumstances," she said, scraping together her tattered pride and daring to look her visitor in the eye. "To avoid its happening again, perhaps in future you'd be so kind as not to show up unannounced in my private quarters."

"Or perhaps in future," a steely masculine voice interrupted from the open garden door, "you wait for an invitation before so much as setting foot on my property, Mother."

Oh, perfect! As if she hadn't been humiliated enough for one morning, now Dario had shown up in time to witness Maeve's near-naked body in all its scrawny glory!

Women of character, she'd once read, always stood their ground and never ran away from a challenge.

She didn't care what women of character did. She fled.

Taking his mother ungently by the elbow, Dario marched her through the garden door and far enough away from the villa that they could not be overheard.

"You are angry," she observed, when at last he released her.

"Angry doesn't begin to cover it, Mother," he informed her in a low, furious tone. "What the devil are you doing here?"

"I assure you my intentions were completely innocent, Dario. I merely dropped in to say hello."

"Innocent, my left foot! You've always got an agenda. Exactly how much did you tell her?"

"Not nearly as much as I might have."

"You had no right to say a word. No right to confront her at all. After everything I've told you, what were you thinking?"

"That I might have misjudged her and, because I knew it would please you, I should give her the chance to redeem herself. And that is all I intended when I came here. But she…! *Madre di Dio,* Dario, she was cavorting naked in the pool. Flaunting herself without a milligram of shame. Can you imagine that?"

All too easily! She'd have looked like a sea nymph. And if he'd been the one to discover her, he'd have stripped off his own clothes and leaped into the pool with her.

Turning aside to hide the smile such an image evoked, he said, "Where's the sin in that?"

"Any one of your staff—a gardener or a housemaid—might have seen her. What do you suppose they would have done?"

"What you should have done, Mother. Disappear. As quickly and discreetly as possible."

She smoothed a fastidious hand over her hair. "Well, since I have no interest in witnessing a repeat performance, I won't disturb her again."

"No, you won't," he assured her, propelling her around to the front of the house and hustling her into her car. "Much though I regret having to take such a drastic step, until such time as the situation with my wife is resolved, you will stick to your own property and stay away from mine."

She lowered the window and pinned him with a reproachful gaze. "I see."

"Do you?" he said, his anger boiling over again. "Do you have any idea, or indeed any interest, in learning of the kind of damage you could have done with your interference? If you had told Maeve about Sebastiano, the consequences could have been disastrous."

"I would never tell her about Sebastiano. If I had my way, she'd be sent packing without ever knowing she bore you a son."

He turned away in disgust. "Which is precisely why you will stay away from her until she recovers her memory."

"And what about you, Dario?" his mother called after him. "Can you stay away from her? Or will you once again fall victim to her cheap, superficial charms and let her entrap you a second time?"

His mother drove away then in a burst of speed that sent crushed rock spraying out from under the car's tires. His harshness had hurt her, he knew, and he wished it could be otherwise. But since he had no intention of allowing her to sabotage his marriage, the change in attitude, if ever there was to be one, had to come from her.

There was no sign of Maeve when he returned to the guest wing. The gate to her garden was closed, and she didn't answer when he knocked on her door. In fact, he neither saw nor heard anything from her until he found her waiting on the terrace to join him for lunch, although *hovering* might have more accurately described her. Wearing a full-skirted dress in varying shades of pink, she resembled a delicate butterfly poised to take flight.

"Nice outfit," he remarked, attempting to lighten the atmosphere, "although I quite liked the towel ensemble, too."

She flushed. "I'm so sorry about that, Dario."

"Why? You're not the one who showed up uninvited. My mother is."

"Still, I wish I'd made a better impression. As it is, I'm afraid I've reinforced her already poor opinion of me. What did I do to make her dislike me so much?"

"You married me," he said, pouring them each an aperitif from the decanter on the sideboard. "Italian mammas always have a hard time accepting their sons' wives. She'll change her attitude when she gets to know you better."

"Perhaps when we have children of our own?"

He choked on his wine. "Possibly," he managed, when he was able to draw breath again, "but there'll be time enough to worry about that when you're feeling yourself again."

"I suppose." She frowned and chewed her lip. "I've been thinking a lot since last night."

In his opinion, she was thinking altogether too much, but saying so wasn't likely to stop her. "About what?"

"You mentioned you oversee the North American side of your family's business. Does that include Canada?"

"It does," he admitted, already uncomfortable with the direction the conversation was taking.

"Have you ever been to Vancouver? Is that where we met?"

"I've been to Vancouver, yes," he said guardedly. "But no, we didn't meet there."

"Then where?"

He hesitated. Less than ten minutes in her company and already he was picking his way through that metaphorical minefield again. "You were on holiday in Italy."

"Alone?"

"No. With a woman friend."

"Where in Italy?"

"Portofino."

"Were you on holiday, as well?"

"You could say so. I keep my yacht moored in the harbor and often used to spend summer weekends there." Carousing the night away with friends, but she didn't need to know that.

"Before you married me, you mean?"

Definitely before he married her! "That's right."

"And we met on your yacht? That's hard to picture. What was I doing there?"

"You weren't. You were in the casino." He grinned as her expression changed from skeptical to outright appalled. "At the roulette table."

"That's even harder to believe. I've never been a gambler."

She wasn't that night, either, which was why he'd been able to lure her away and ply her with enough champagne to loosen her inhibitions. Profligate that he'd been back then, he'd thought it would be amusing to give such a lovely young thing a night to remember. What he hadn't bargained on was finding himself tied to her for life.

CHAPTER FIVE

HE'D noticed her at once. Needing nothing more than pearls and a straight, strapless gown in basic black to enhance her blond beauty, she carried herself with the grace and dignity of a duchess. But what captured his interest was less her elegance and style than the indifference in her blue eyes when she caught him looking at her. He wasn't accustomed to being ignored by the opposite sex, especially not on his recreational home turf.

The woman with her, flamboyant in feathers and crimson ruffles, more accurately portrayed the kind of tourist found in the casinos—which was to say, wearing too much jewelry and attracting attention to herself by working too hard at having a good time. "Save my place, Maeve," she squealed, raking in her pile of chips. "I'm off to powder my nose."

"Is that really what women do?" he said, moving into the spot she vacated.

The duchess spared him a lofty glance. "I beg your pardon?"

"Do women really still powder their noses?"

"I have no idea," she replied stiffly. "I don't make a habit of asking them. And by the way, that seat is taken."

"By your friend." He nodded. "Yes, I heard. I'll hold it for her until she returns." Then, as a new game began, went on, "Are you not placing any bets?"

"No. I'm here to keep Pamela company, and don't have any chips."

He slid a pile of his own in front of her. "You do now."

She shied away as if he'd thrust a loaded pistol at her, and wrinkled her dainty nose. "I can't possibly take yours. For heaven's sake, I don't even know you. You could be anyone."

Both amused and piqued by her unsophisticated candor, he said with as much solemnity as he could manage, "I'm Dario Costanzo and perfectly respectable, as *anyone* here will tell you."

Not missing his deliberate emphasis on the word, she blushed disarmingly. "I wasn't trying to be offensive."

"I'm sure you weren't."

"Even so, I can't accept your money."

"It isn't money until you win."

Very firmly, she returned his chips to him. "Which I'm not likely to do since I haven't a clue how the game is played."

"I could teach you."

"No, thank you."

He eyed her thoughtfully. "You're not enjoying yourself much, are you?"

"No," she admitted. "This isn't my kind of place. I wouldn't be here at all if it weren't for my friend."

"What is your kind of place?"

"Somewhere quieter and less crowded."

"Come with me. I know the perfect spot."

She shot down that suggestion with a glance that would

have turned a less determined man to stone. "I don't think so, thank you!"

"Because you're still worried that I might be the local ax murderer?"

She pressed her lips together, but wasn't quite able to hide her smile. "The thought has crossed my mind."

"Then allow me to put your fears to rest." He signaled the manager, a man in his late fifties who epitomized silver-haired respectability and whom he'd known for years. "Federico, would you be so kind as to vouch for me to this young lady? She's not sure I'm to be trusted."

Federico straightened his impeccably clad shoulders. "Signor Costanzo is one of our most valued clients, *signora,*" he told her, subtly conveying shock than anyone might assume otherwise. "I speak from long and personal experience when I say you find yourself in excellent company."

"Well?" Dario eyed her questioningly as the man departed. "Did that change your mind at all?"

She flinched at a sudden burst of raucous laughter behind her. "I admit I'd be tempted to take you up on your offer if it weren't for Pamela. I can't just abandon her."

But Pamela, as he pointed out, had found diversion at the next table with a man old enough to be her father. "Sure," she brayed, flapping her beringed hand as if dismissing an annoying fly when the duchess stopped by to mention she was leaving. "See you whenever, but probably not before tomorrow. I have big plans for tonight."

And so, Dario thought, had he. Increasingly intrigued by the duchess's cool reserve, he ushered her out of the casino. "Shall we stroll for a while?"

"I'd love to," she said, breathing deeply of the balmy night air. "I found it unbearably stuffy inside."

Although his ultimate goal was to lure her aboard the yacht, he took her first to a tiny supper club tucked away in a quiet corner of *la piazzetta*. A frequent visitor, he was shown immediately to one of the candlelit tables on the covered patio.

"Better?" he inquired.

"Much," she sighed, slipping out of her evening sandals and wiggling her bare toes.

More charmed by the minute, he undid his black bow tie and the top button of his dress shirt, ordered champagne cocktails, and encouraged her to talk about herself.

The wine loosened her tongue and in short order he learned her name was Maeve Montgomery and she was from Vancouver, Canada. After two years in college, she'd worked as a sales assistant in a bridal salon, been promoted to fashion director at the ripe old age of twenty-two, but found her true calling when she became a personal shopper for clients long on money, but short on taste. She was an unapologetic clothes horse, sewed many of her own outfits and lived in a sixth-floor apartment with a west-facing view of Georgia Strait and the Gulf Islands.

She'd been very close to her parents, both of whom had died within the past five years. Her father, never sick a day in his life, had suffered a ruptured abdominal aneurysm as he sat watching television. He was gone in less time than it took to phone for an ambulance. Thirty-four months later her mother, a severe asthmatic, had succumbed to pneumonia at age seventy. "I miss them dreadfully," she confessed.

That she was in Italy at all had been a last-minute arrangement and a bonus of sorts from Mrs. Samuel Elliott-Rhys, a grateful, longtime client who happened also to be Pamela's mother. "The friend who was supposed to come with Pamela slipped and broke her leg the week before last," Maeve explained. "Mrs. Elliott-Rhys persuaded me to take the friend's place because she wasn't comfortable having Pamela traveling alone."

I wouldn't be, either, if Pamela were my daughter, Dario thought, but declined to say so. After all, he had her to thank for the way the evening was turning out. "How much longer will you be in Portofino?"

"Five days. We fly home next Wednesday."

Perfect! Enough time for an enjoyable fling, without the entanglement of her expecting a lasting association. "More champagne?" he suggested smoothly.

"I don't think so, thanks. I don't like to drink too much."

She'd had two glasses only. "Can one ever have too much of a good thing?"

"Maybe not, but if it's all the same to you, I'd rather walk some more before I have anything else."

"By all means." He pulled back her chair and knelt to slip her narrow, elegant feet into her shoes.

They set off again, along the cobbled promenade toward the harbor. She didn't object when, as they approached the ramp leading down to the docks, he held her hand firmly and said, "Be careful. Those high heels weren't designed for this kind of walking, and I'd hate to see you trip."

"I'm more concerned about getting arrested," she confided, taking in the flotilla of expensive yachts at anchor in the bay. "Are you sure it's okay for us to be wandering around like this?"

"Perfectly. I keep my own boat here."

"If it's anything like these others, I'm way out of my league."

"Don't let them intimidate you. Most are charters," he said, but didn't bother to add that his was larger than any she'd yet seen and never available for charter. She was antsy enough as it was.

He always anchored as far from the docks as possible, a smart decision in more ways than one. When he felt inclined to go sailing, he was soon clear of the harbor and into open water. When he had seduction in mind, he was assured of privacy. And tonight he definitely had seduction in mind.

As soon as she was seated in the dinghy he kept moored at the end of the last dock, he fired up the outboard engine and sped across the water to the big boat. Once aboard, he wasted no time setting the mood. A little champagne, a little soft music. Just enough lantern glow on the promenade deck to compensate for the absence of moonlight. Precisely the right kind of casual conversation to put her at ease.

No, he didn't live on the yacht, but did spend days at a time cruising the Mediterranean with friends. Yes, being able to get away from it all helped him unwind. He'd take her out tomorrow, if she liked—let her experience the pleasure for herself. Meanwhile, would she like to dance?

"If I can go barefoot," she said.

She could go stark naked if she wanted to, but again he refrained from voicing his opinion aloud. The night was still relatively young. Time enough to think about undressing her later. "Of course," he said, and took her in his arms.

At first, she held herself a little stiffly, but he'd selected the music well. Trendier names might top the charts these days, but as far as he was concerned, if romantic ambience was on the menu, nothing could beat the melodies of the legendary Nat King Cole.

At six-two, Dario was taller than most Italians, but Maeve was tall, too, close to five-nine, he'd guess, and that was without the heels. It made for a stimulating fit of male and female anatomy. As the timeless magic of the music wound around them, she relaxed enough to let him mold her body to his. Her hair smelled of bergamot and thyme. Her skin was as soft and warm as a sun-kissed gardenia petal.

He slid his hand to the small of her back and deliberately urged her closer still. Close enough that she couldn't miss the erection he made no attempt to hide. He felt the accelerated puff of her breath through his shirt front, the wild flutter of her lashes against his cheek.

The music died. Tilting her face up to his, he held her captive in his gaze. Across the water a ship's bell sounded, haunting and soulful. As it, too, faded, he let the silence spin out just long enough to stoke the sexual tension arcing between them so that, when at last he kissed her, she melted in his arms.

Never one to rush his pleasures—and without question she promised pure, unadulterated pleasure—he backed her under the canvas awning, which offered utter seclusion from prying eyes, and kissed her again. At her temple and her ear. Down her throat to the hollow of her shoulder. Then hearing her murmur his name on a sigh of entreaty, he brought his mouth again to hers. Felt it soften beneath his and knew victory lay within his grasp.

Still he lingered. Why hurry to sample the entire feast

when the night lay ahead, inviting him to savor each course at leisure?

Her arms stole around his neck. He kissed her again, more deeply this time, and ran his tongue lightly over the seam of her lips. They parted softly, allowing him access to the secrets of her mouth. She tasted of champagne. Intoxicating, irresistible. And he wanted more of her. Lots more.

Stealthily he unzipped her gown. It slithered the length of her to puddle blackly around her ankles. She wore no bra, and panties so brief and flimsy that even he, who thought he understood all the mysteries women's lingerie had to offer, wasn't sure how she held them up. His finger hooked inside the elasticized strip at her hips, and with one slight tug disposed of the scrap of fabric.

Appearing almost dazed, she obediently stepped out of the heap of silk clinging to her ankles and submitted herself to his awed inspection. Fully clothed she had been beautiful. Naked she was breathtaking. Long legged, narrow-waisted, sweetly curved. Pure symmetry of form encased in skin as smooth as cream and lustrous as the pearls at her throat. And suddenly, feasting his eyes on her wasn't enough. He wanted all of her and he wanted her now with an urgency that should have embarrassed him.

Any attempt at leisurely seduction shot to blazes, he stripped off his own clothes with unpolished haste and tossed them in a heap beside hers on the deck. He'd planned to kiss every inch of her until she begged him to lay full claim to her. Instead, he found himself begging her, his voice hoarse with need as he urged her to touch him as intimately as he was touching her.

She did so tentatively, her fingers skimming shyly down his belly and closing around him with such exquisite care that he almost came, when what he'd planned, what he hoped, was first to bring her to orgasm with his tongue.

It wasn't going to happen, not this time. He teetered too close to the edge of destruction to postpone the inevitable, and it was either make a complete ass of himself, or take her now and pray he could last long enough to give her some satisfaction.

He chose the latter. Lowering her to the cushioned seat, he straddled her and pushed her legs apart with his knee. In a moment of madness, he teased her flesh with the tip of his penis, nudging himself against her for the pure pleasure of feeling her silken heat against his unprotected skin. Her scent rose, dark and sweet, a drugging combination so erotic that he barely had time to roll on a condom before driving into her.

Unexpectedly, he met with faint but unmistakable resistance. He heard her tiny whimper and felt the brief, convulsive clutch of her hands at his shoulders. They told him all he needed to know, and if he'd possessed a shred of integrity, he'd have stopped then. But he'd passed the point of no return. Blind hunger obliterated all sense of decency, he thrust harder, and in a matter of seconds was shuddering within her in helpless release.

And she? *Dio perdonare lui*, she lay trembling beneath him, her eyes wide dark pools in the dim light.

"Mi displace," he muttered, when he could speak again, and stroked his hand down her cheek. "Maeve, I'm sorry… I had no idea…!"

She turned her face and pressed a kiss into his palm. "Don't be," she whispered. "I'm glad you were the one."

Cursing himself with every foul expletive at his command, he went below deck and returned a minute later, wearing a terry cloth robe and bringing another for her. Wrapping it around her, he scooped her onto his lap. "How are you feeling? Did I hurt you?"

"Not really, no." She curled up in his arms like a child.

Except she wasn't a child—or was she? How was a man to tell these days, with girls of fourteen dressing and behaving like adults? Gripped by fresh consternation, he asked the question begging to be answered. "How old are you, Maeve?"

"Twenty-eight."

He expelled a sigh of relief laced with astonishment. "And until tonight you were a virgin?"

"Yes. I've never had the time for a serious relationship."

A different kind of alarm swept over him then. Did she think making love equaled a serious relationship? Surely not. At twenty-eight she couldn't be that far out of touch with reality. "A woman's first time should be special," he said. "I must have disappointed you."

"No. I'll remember this night for as long as I live."

So would he, but not for the reasons she supposed. He couldn't recall the last time he'd been so rattled. "And a very long night it's been, too. You must be exhausted." He slid her off his lap and picked up her dress and the ridiculous panties. "I'll show you where you can get dressed, then take you back to your hotel."

"Oh…yes. All right."

Refusing to acknowledge the disappointment he heard in her voice, he showed her to a guest stateroom and stuffed her clothes in after her. "No need to rush. I'll wait for you on deck."

He had the outboard running when she reappeared, and wasted no time whisking her ashore. He couldn't wait to be rid of her. Not because, having had his way with her, he'd lost all interest, but because he felt lower than dirt and hardly knew how to face her.

She was staying at the Splendido Mare. He walked her as far as the front entrance, but made no move to go inside with her. He wasn't about to risk having her invite him up to her room. He wasn't sure he'd be able to say no. "Thank you for a very special evening, sweet Maeve," he said, kissing her on both cheeks. "Sleep well, and *buona notte*."

He'd already turned away when she called out, "What time shall I see you tomorrow?"

"Tomorrow?" He spun back toward her.

"Yes. You said you'd take me out for a spin on your yacht, remember?"

Unfortunately, he did, and if she'd been any other woman, he'd have come up with an excuse to rescind the invitation, but she was looking at him with such artless anticipation that he hadn't the heart to dash her hopes. "Let's say two o'clock at the marina."

"Wonderful. I'll see you then."

The radiance of her smile shamed him even further. *"Sì,"* he mumbled. *"A domani."*

By the time she showed up the next afternoon, he'd rounded up a small group of friends to join them, and brought his crew onboard to ferry passengers back and forth and serve drinks and meals. Safety in numbers and all that, he'd reasoned.

Once her initial shyness wore off, she seemed to enjoy herself. Certainly none of the others would have guessed she wasn't part of the in crowd. However humble her background, she looked and acted as if she'd been born to high society.

"I like your friends," she said, lacing her fingers in his when, after dinner served on the same deck where he'd deflowered her less than twenty-four hours earlier, he found himself alone with her. Most likely in a misguided effort to give the pair of them some privacy, his other guests had drifted over to stand at the rail. "Thank you for introducing me to them. I feel I know you so much better now."

Oh, *inferno!* That hadn't been the message he'd intended to get across. "You've made quite an impression on them, too, especially Eduardo," he said, knowing he could count on his old friend to back him up in this. They went back a long way and had helped each other out of similar awkward situations more than once in the past. "Don't be surprised if he wants to see you again before you leave."

"As if I'd agree to that!"

"Well, why not? He knows more about the history of the area than anyone you could ask to meet, and can show you places never mentioned in the guide books."

"And you wouldn't object?" she asked, looking woebegone as a lost puppy.

"I'd have no right. I don't own you."

Her face fell. "No, of course not." She patted his hand and reached for her straw beach bag. "Listen, Dario, I think I've had a touch too much sun and feel a headache coming on, so if you don't mind, I'm going to slip away quietly and call it a night."

"Are you sure?"

"Oh, quite," she said, leaving him in no doubt he'd got his message across loud and clear.

"In that case, I'll take you ashore." It was, he figured, the least he could do, especially as the crew was occupied clearing away the remains of dinner.

She didn't speak again until he tied up at the dock and handed her out of the dinghy. Then, fending him off as he went to accompany her up the ramp, she said, "That's far enough. I can manage on my own now."

He might be a cad, but he wasn't entirely without chivalry. "Nonsense. I insist on seeing you safely back at the hotel."

"No." She shook her head. "There's no need to keep up the pretense. I'm not a child, Dario, and although I probably strike you as pitifully unsophisticated, I'm not completely naive. You've had your fun with me, and now it's over. I get it."

Shame, thick and bitter, coated his tongue. "I'm not sure I know how you expect me to respond to that," he muttered.

"Then let me make it easy for you. We made love or had sex or however you choose to describe it, by mutual consent. It was a one-night stand or a short-lived holiday romance, again depending on your point of view. And since that's all it was, let's chalk it up to its being just one of those things, and say goodbye with no hard feelings."

She might be sexually inexperienced, but she was a pro when it came to making a man feel lower than a worm. "If I've deceived you, Maeve, and clearly you think I have, then I'm sorry. In my own defense, however, I have to say you deceived me also, even if you never intended to."

"Because I didn't warn you ahead of time that I was a virgin, you mean?"

"Yes."

"Would it have made any difference if I had?"

"All the difference in the world," he said gently. "I would never have laid a hand on you, no matter how desirable I found you."

She blinked back a tear. "I never thought I'd come to regret saving myself until the right man came along."

"That's my whole point, *cara*. Sadly, I'm not the right man for you, at least not long-term."

"And I'm not cut out to be some rich playboy's toy." She wiped her eyes and leaned forward to kiss his cheek. "Goodbye, Dario. Thank you for everything," she said, and quickly walked away.

She was wrong, he thought regretfully, curbing the urge to run after her as she disappeared. He did not see women as toys. He had the utmost respect for them and, for the most part, had remained on good terms with his former lovers.

He did, however, look for a certain level of sophistication in those he took to bed. He was straightforward and did not make promises he had no intention of keeping. When an affair had run its course, he expected his partners to accept the end gracefully. No histrionics, no tearful protestations of undying love, no public scenes.

For that reason the charming ingenue was not for him. At least, she hadn't been until Maeve Montgomery had shown up in his life.

CHAPTER SIX

"DARIO?"

He blinked and shook his head, as though trying to throw off the effects of sleep. "Sorry," he mumbled. "Did you say something?"

"I'm wondering where you went to, just now. One minute you were here, the next, you were gone. Lost in thought."

"I was remembering," he said.

Lucky him! She wished she could. "Remembering what?"

"Nothing special."

"Nothing pleasant, either, if the look on your face is any indication. Are you going to tell me about it?"

"No," he said. "You wouldn't be interested."

"Why don't you let me be the judge of that?"

Draining his glass, he strode to the sideboard and removed the heavy glass stopper from the decanter. "I haven't used the yacht in months," he said, pouring himself another aperitif, "and was thinking I should get someone to check and make sure everything's ship-shape on board."

She no more believed him than she believed the moon was made of green cheese, but the set of his shoulders and the stubborn cast to his mouth told her she'd get nowhere by saying so. Clearly, as far as he was concerned, the subject was closed.

For now, maybe. But not for long. Not if she had any say in the matter.

The next several days passed uneventfully. Too uneventfully. Although attentive and pleasant when they were together, which wasn't nearly often enough in Maeve's opinion, Dario deftly turned aside any attempt on her part to get him to reveal details of their shared past.

He wasn't quite as reticent about his life and background before he'd known her. His parents set great store by education, he told her, and their children had not disappointed them. He'd earned an MBA from Harvard; his elusive sister had a degree in art history from the Sorbonne. And if that wasn't academic glory enough to satisfy them, his brother-in-law was a graduate of the London School of Economics.

Small wonder his mother was so hostile, Maeve thought when she heard all this. A diploma in sales from the local community college, which was all the foreign wife could bring to the table, didn't stack up too well beside such impressive credentials.

Had he arrived at the same conclusion and decided he'd made a mistake in marrying her? she wondered. Was that what lay behind her nagging sense of impending doom, and why he never kissed her again as he had that first evening?

The most he'd permitted himself since was a chaste peck on both her cheeks when he bade her good-night. The rest of the time, he kept his distance both physically and emotionally. Once in a while, she thought she saw the subdued light of desire smoldering in his gaze as he sat across the candlelit dinner table from her, but he always managed to dampen it when he realized she was observing him.

When she wasn't with him, she could have set her watch by the fixed routine that marked the passing hours. She slept late, ate breakfast by herself in her suite, swam in her private pool, lolled in the endless sun on her private terrace and either played solitaire or thumbed through the magazines on the coffee table in her private sitting room until she met him for lunch.

In the afternoon she napped for an hour or two, swam and lazed some more. At four o'clock she was served Earl Grey tea in china cups so translucent, she could practically read print through them, and *mostazzoli panteschi,* intricate little pastries filled with sweetened semolina, which the cook baked specially for her because she happened to mention once how much she liked them.

In fact, no matter how discontented she might be about other aspects of her "new" life, food was the one thing she couldn't fault. Meals were invariably delicious, an extravaganza of island specialties: fresh seafood, capers in a variety of sauces and salads, pasta, an abundance of exotic fruit and wonderful desserts made with honey and almonds. Enough of those and she'd soon put back the pounds she'd lost—and then some. That Dario managed to remain so fit and trim was simply one more unresolved mystery.

As twilight fell, she went about the business of making herself look presentable for the coming evening with a mixture of anticipation and dread. Would this be the night her memory returned and she discovered why she sometimes felt a sense of loss so acute that it left her sick to her stomach?

But it never was, and she was back in bed no later than ten-thirty or eleven, at the mercy of an exhaustion she couldn't overcome. Or was it that she sought escape in sleep so as not to have to acknowledge the demons hounding her when she was awake?

Questions. Always questions. And never any answers.

Apart from joining her at lunch and in the evening, Dario spent most of his time on the phone or glued to the computer in his study, keeping abreast of developments in the company's head office, or consulting on business-related matters with those members of the family who were also in residence on the island. At least, she assumed that's why around the same time every day he'd disappear for an hour or so. But all she really knew for sure was that, wherever he went, he never invited her to accompany him.

Not that she was ever left alone. The household staff smothered her with attention. About the only thing they didn't offer to do was hold her hand while she went to the toilet.

Finally she'd had enough and confronted him at lunch, the Wednesday after she arrived on the island.

He gave her the perfect opening. "I have to fly up to the city tomorrow," he said, fixing them each a campari and soda.

"You're going to Milan?" Her heart lifted at the prospect of escaping this place and the dark, overwhelming air of sadness that so often hounded her. To be around other people who didn't look at her as if she wasn't quite all there, to get her hair styled, instead of snipping at it herself with a pair of manicure scissors, that would be bliss! "Good. I'll come with you."

"No," he said flatly. "The pace of the city's much too frantic. You're supposed to stay quiet and take it easy."

"But if we have a penthouse there—"

"We have an entire house here, and I'll be gone only a couple of days, or as long as it takes me to attend a few meetings. I don't need the distraction of worrying about what you're up to when I'm in the middle of sensitive business negotiations."

Annoyed by his autocratic refusal, she said, "And what am I supposed to do while you're away, Dario? There's nothing here to keep me occupied."

"You can relax, recuperate—"

"I've done nothing but relax and recuperate for the past several weeks, not to mention being comatose for a whole month before that, and frankly I'm tired of it. I'm marking time when what I want is to pick up my life where I left it off."

He shrugged. "You already are. You're back home with your husband. Can't you let that be enough for now?"

"No, because there's something missing."

"If you're talking about us and our present living arrangement, I can't imagine you want to engage in marital relations with a man you don't remember marrying."

Actually, that wasn't quite true. She might have no memory of *when* she married him, but the more she saw of him, the better she understood *why*. His smile left her weak at the knees. His voice reverberated throughout her body with the deep, exotic resonance of a jungle drum. As for his touch, whether he intended it to be so or not, it turned her insides to a molten lava that rivaled anything the island volcanoes had ever produced.

But there was more to him than pure sex appeal. She'd soon seen beyond the striking good looks to the intelligence, the integrity, the decency. A man half as attractive would have been insulted that his wife didn't remember him. But Dario continued to treat her with the utmost patience and respect, asking nothing more than that she enjoy herself and get well again.

Misreading her introspection, he said, "Don't think it's easy, living in the same house with you, Maeve, and not giving in to my baser instincts. I'm a man, not a saint."

Oh, hallelujah! She wasn't the only one lying alone in bed every night and wishing it were otherwise. But, "There's more to it than that," she confessed. "Something I can't quite put my finger on." Her voice broke and she pressed a clenched fist to her heart. "I feel a deep emptiness here that nothing, not even you, can fill. I have, ever since I set foot in this house."

Quickly setting down his glass, he pulled her into the curve of his arm and stroked her back. "Because you're pushing yourself too hard and letting frustration get the better of you."

"Can you blame me?" She tugged free of his hold, not about to be swayed from her original course by her runaway hormones. "There's a limit to how much mollycoddling I can take, and I've reached it."

"You're not enjoying being taken care of?"

"Did Napoleon enjoy being exiled on Elba?"

"You're not a prisoner, *mio dolce*."

"I might as well be. I can't blink without someone taking note of the fact, and as for wanting to roam freely about the house the way any other wife would, or discuss menus with the cook, forget it! It's not my place to do any such thing. I'm essentially confined to barracks unless I'm with you. It's like living in boot camp!"

He laughed, so relaxed and charming that she knew if she didn't keep her wits about her, she was in danger of finding him even more adorable than she already did. "Oh, not quite that bad, surely?"

Worse, in fact. She was treated like visiting royalty. And therein lay the problem. She wasn't a visitor, she was the mistress of the house. Or at least she was supposed to be. But the one time she'd ventured as far as the kitchen, the cook had descended on her, clucking like an overwrought hen, and shooed her away.

"It sometimes feels that way. Take today, for instance. Because I was dressed and ready for lunch early, instead of doing as I usually do and sticking to my own little garden, I decided to wander farther afield and explore the rest of the grounds to see if something—anything—might jog my memory.

"First, I practically had to wrestle my way past a maid who didn't think I should be allowed through the front door. Then, once I was outside, no matter which way I turned, I kept running into people—gardeners, maintenance men, you name it—who made it clear I shouldn't wander off the main paths or go too close to the edge of the cliff. So I went down the drive, thinking I'd take a walk along the road, and got as far as the gates only to find them locked. When I asked one of the workers why, he pretended he didn't understand me, even though I spoke to him in Italian."

"Not surprising." Turning away, Dario busied himself re-filling his glass. "He speaks the local dialect, which is quite different from anything you hear on the mainland. Even native Italians have trouble communicating with the islanders. Another campari and soda?"

Refusing to let him distract her, she shook her head. "No, thanks. Look, I can see why you'd want to keep strangers from wandering all over your property, but surely those of us living here should be able to get out if we feel like it? Why, even the door in my garden wall is now kept locked."

"I know. I ordered it to preserve your privacy after my mother's unscheduled visit."

"The point I'm making," she went on, doggedly ignoring the interruption, "is that I've been here almost a week, and to put it bluntly, I'm suffocating. I step out of my suite, and a maid immediately shows up to escort me to wherever I'm supposed to go next. I try to familiarize myself with my surroundings, and I'm stymied at every turn. I feel like a hamster running endlessly on a wheel, but never getting anywhere."

"Then how about this?" he said soothingly. "I'll take the afternoon off and, after lunch, we'll tour the island by boat. If you feel up to it, we can even stop in your favorite cove and go snorkeling. Would you like that?"

She'd like it better if he'd just be straight with her, instead of stalling for time. Before he'd squelched it, she'd seen the brief flash of dismay in his eyes when she'd mentioned the emptiness inside, and guessed he knew exactly what caused it. And if he thought a dip in the sea would be enough to wash it from her thoughts, he was mistaken. Either he gave her the answers she sought, or she'd find someone who would.

On the other hand, after whining about boredom and lack of freedom, she could hardly turn down his invitation to do something different, and visiting a place that had meant something to her in the past might prove to be the key that would unlock her mind.

"Yes, I would," she said, swallowing her frustration and doing her best to sound suitably appeased. "Thank you."

* * *

Viewing Pantelleria by boat instead of from the air gave her a whole new perspective on the island. In places, giant cliffs swept down to isolated pockets of pebble beach. In others, great outcroppings of purple-black lava rose up from the cobalt Mediterranean to encircle dreamy lagoons.

Montagna Grande, towering nearly three thousand feet above sea level, stood guard over bright green fertile valleys crisscrossed with ancient stone walls. In other areas, the softer gray-green of low-growing juniper, heather and myrtle that Dario said was called *macchia,* ran wild over the land. "The scent when the wind blows from the west is enough to knock your head off," he told her.

They sailed past isolated farms and a tiny fishing village where water bubbled up from the thermal springs in its harbor. Another village clung to the edge of a sheer cliff, with glorious views across the sea. But awe inspiring though all that was, the spectacle much closer at hand stirred Maeve's blood more.

Dario in tailored black trousers and white shirt was a sight that would kick any woman's heart rate up a notch. But Dario in swimming trunks, with the wind ruffling his hair, was enough to stop a woman's pulse altogether.

Seated beside him in the eighteen-foot Donzi runabout, Maeve had to keep reminding herself that this man really was her husband, and of all the women in the world he might have chosen, he'd picked her to be his wife.

His bronzed torso gleamed in the sun. The only shadows came from the play of muscle in his forearms as he effortlessly navigated Pantelleria's jagged coastline. The hands loosely gripping the steering wheel were strong and capable. Once, they had touched her intimately. She knew it, even though she couldn't remember when, because looking at them sent a spasm of awareness shooting through her body.

And his mouth—had it done the same thing? Or was the sudden damp flood at her core brought on by wishful thinking?

Catching her inspecting him and quite misunderstanding the reason, he grinned and said, "Relax, Maeve, I know what I'm doing. We're not going to run aground."

"I wasn't watching you," she said, rolling truth and fib together into a seamless whole. "I was admiring the view."

"Then you're facing the wrong way." Shifting the throttle so that the boat idled in Neutral, he lifted his arm and pointed off the starboard bow. "Look over there."

She turned and let out a gasp of delight. No more than twenty yards away, a pod of dolphins frolicked in the turquoise water. "I would give the world to be like them," she breathed, entranced. "They're everything I wish I was. Playful, graceful, beautiful."

"You're beautiful, Maeve. I told you so the first night you came home again, and nothing's changed my mind since then."

"No, you don't understand. I'm not fishing for compliments, I'm talking about their spirit. They embody a joie de vivre I seem to have lost. I'm in limbo—a stranger inside my own skin."

"Not to me," he murmured, for once leaning so close that his breath teased the outer rim of her ear. "You're the woman I married."

She leaned against him, loving his closeness, the heat of his body, the scent of his sun-kissed skin. Loving him. "Tell me about that—about our getting married, I mean. Did we have a big wedding?"

He hesitated just long enough for a shiver of apprehension to steal over her. "No. It was a very quiet, intimate affair."

"Why?"

Again that ominous pause before he said, "Because we were married in Vancouver. I could spare only a few days before returning to Italy, which made planning an elaborate affair out of the question."

"So it was a spur-of-the-moment thing?"

"More or less. I took you by surprise, and popped the question, to coin the rather odd English way of putting it. You had just enough time to run out and find a dress to wear."

"What color?"

"Blue," he said. "The same shade as your eyes."

"And flowers?"

"You carried a small bouquet of white lilies and roses."

"My favorites!"

"Yes."

"Who else was there?"

"Two witnesses. A former colleague of yours whose name I don't recall, and a business associate of mine."

"Did we have rings?"

"Yes. White-gold wedding bands, yours studded with diamonds."

"Where are they now?"

"The clinic administrator gave yours to me for safekeeping."

"What about a honeymoon?"

"Just four short days on the yacht. I couldn't spare more time."

She splayed the fingers of her left hand across her knee. "I think I'd like to wear my ring again. Is it at the house?"

"No. It's with mine, in the penthouse safe, in Milan. I'll get them both the next time I'm in the city." He slid back behind the wheel and put the engine in gear again. "For now, we have more to do and see out here."

Slowly they continued their tour of the island, and finally, with the worst heat of the day past, he guided the Donzi between upthrust spears of basalt rock and dropped anchor in a quiet, secluded cove.

Donning masks, snorkels and fins, they slipped over the side of the boat and drifted facedown over water teeming with marine life. Schools of black-and-orange-striped fish darted among the coral beds. Red starfish, their color made all the more vivid by contrast, clung to dark volcanic rock. Tiny crustaceans scuttled into the protection of miniature forests of algae the likes of which, as far as she knew, she'd never seen before. Close to the mouth of the cove, she came across the remains of an ancient amphora, relic of a shipwreck that had taken place centuries before.

When, after more than an hour in the water, they at last climbed aboard the runabout again, the sun had slipped low on the western horizon. Tired, content and wrapped in a huge beach towel, she snuggled close to Dario as he weighed anchor and set the Donzi on its homeward course.

As usual, that evening they dined on the terrace, or *ducchena* as Dario had taught her to call it. Maeve dressed with particular care before joining him. Much though she'd enjoyed the afternoon, it hadn't produced the results she'd hoped for. She had no more recollection of visiting the cove previously than she had of marrying Dario, and she was determined that not another night would pass without her making some sort of progress. If that meant having to seduce him into revealing all he knew, then that's what she was prepared to do. It was a case of the ends justifying the means, although why justification should be necessary was a moot point. He was her husband, after all, and had more or less admitted he'd grown as weary of celibacy as she had.

Inspecting the more formal dinner dresses in her closet, none of which she'd yet worn, she rejected the first two, which, though lovely, weren't as eye-catching as the third, a silk charmeuse in deepest jade-green, with a high empire waistline. In contrast to the modesty of the softly flared long sleeves, the low-cut neckline could be described as nothing short of daring. A huge pearl buckle centered below the bust brought together the artfully draped fabric of the bodice, and released it in a free fall of dramatic, shimmering color almost to her ankles. Simple but sophisticated, it required only a pair of teardrop pearl earrings and high-heeled black sandals to complement it.

"Lei è una visione, mia bella," Dario said reverently, when he saw her.

She cast him a deliberately provocative glance from beneath demurely lowered eyelashes. "Thank you."

That she'd achieved the effect she'd been hoping for was immediately apparent. He almost missed the flutes he was filling and came close to splashing vintage champagne all over his shoes.

Recovering himself, he gestured to the sun chaises and said solicitously, "You must have found this afternoon very tiring. Why don't you put your feet up while we wait for dinner to be served?"

The chaises were separated by a low table that allowed for no body contact, but down by the pool was a canopied patio swing built for two. "Why don't we have our drinks on the lower deck, for a change?" she suggested, running a deliberate fingertip from the top of her plunging neckline to her cleavage. "The pool looks so lovely in the moonlight. It reminds me of a huge cabochon sapphire."

Eyeing her suspiciously, he shrugged. "*Certo*. Whatever pleases you. But take my arm going down the steps. You might trip in those heels otherwise."

For a brief, startling second, she forgot her plans to seduce him as another flower-scented night, and a narrow street paved with uneven cobblestones illuminated by streetlamps, flashed before her eyes. And then, as quickly as it appeared, the picture was gone. Imagination? she wondered, her pulse jumping. Or a bone fide memory slipping through the layers clouding her mind?

There was only one way to find out. "I seem to recall your saying that to me before."

He laughed and tucked her hand beneath his elbow. "Only about a hundred times."

"Why? I know I made a practice of falling over my own feet when I was a teenager, but I'd hoped I'm not quite as clumsy anymore."

"You aren't," he assured her. "You're one of the most graceful women I've ever met. But that doesn't mean I shouldn't go out of my way to keep you safe."

They'd reached the pool deck by then. Not waiting for him to suggest they occupy any of the several chaises lined up around its perimeter, she slipped her hand free of his arm and wandered ever so casually to the swing, leaving him with little choice but to follow and sit down next to her. "Where were you, then, the day of my accident?" she asked.

Even though he wasn't quite touching her, she felt the sudden tension emanating from his body as acutely as if static electricity had leaped between them. "Obviously not doing my job."

"I'm not blaming you, Dario," she amended hurriedly. "No one can be expected to look out for someone else all the time, especially not an adult who should be able to look out for herself."

"But I do blame myself," he said, his voice raw.

She opened her mouth to refute such a notion, then closed it again as another thought occurred. "Oh, dear!" she exclaimed softly. "Are you telling me you were driving the car, and hold yourself responsible for my injuries? Is that why you won't talk to me about it?"

He swung around to face her with such leashed anger that she flinched. "No. If I'd been at the wheel, you never would have been hurt and…"

"And what?"

"And we wouldn't be sitting here like this."

"Like what?"

"Brother and sister," he exploded. "Good friends. Polite strangers. Take your pick."

"You don't like our status quo?"

"What do you take me for?" he ground out. "Of course I don't like our status quo! What red-blooded man would?"

She inched closer until her thigh touched his, and put her hand on his knee. "Then why don't you do something about it, Dario?" she said.

CHAPTER SEVEN

HE'D never thought to see the day or night that he would turn down a beautiful, sexy woman's advances. But when he'd married Maeve, he'd cast aside his role of quintessential playboy and relied on his moral compass to make a success of a union he'd neither anticipated nor wanted. The same inborn sense of decency kicked in now, reining in his response to her.

"Because I'm not convinced you know what you're asking for," he said.

She cupped his jaw and turned his face to hers. "Will this change your mind?" she whispered, her sweetly fragrant breath feathering over his lips to infiltrate his mouth.

At once bold and hungry, her kiss inflamed his soul. This was the Maeve he'd married, he thought, his senses swimming; the girl in a woman's body whom he'd coaxed into shedding the inhibitions that had dogged her most of her life. He had taught her well. She'd blossomed under his expert tutelage; had reveled in her newfound sexuality. And now she was using it to destroy him.

Still he fought, bolstered by doubts he'd never fully acknowledged before. Who was it she really craved: her husband, or Yves Gauthier, the French-Canadian summer visitor with whom she'd struck up such a close alliance, and in whose rented car she'd been traveling when the accident occurred?

"Until you regain your memory, you don't even know me, Maeve," he said, forcing the words past the strangling constriction in his throat.

"I know I want you, and have ever since last week when I walked down the steps from that jet and into your waiting arms."

Did she? Or was she merely responding to the same wild hormonal attraction that had lured her to surrender her innocence to him in the first place? He wished he knew.

As though sensing his uncertainty, she upped the ante by angling her body so that her breast nudged his biceps. "Please, Dario…"

Cursing inwardly, he closed his eyes against the temptation. Undeterred, she murmured his name again and guided his hand inside her low-cut gown to cradle her fullness. Her nipple surged against his palm, eager and responsive. Unbearably aroused already, he clenched his teeth against the increased onslaught to his stamina.

Impatient with his resistance, and with an abandon that left him reeling, she made a sound deep in her throat and, pulling her skirt up around her waist, moved swiftly to sit astride his lap.

Her long bare legs, pale as ivory in the moonlight and his for the taking, leveled his defenses. He couldn't help himself. He touched her, skimming his palms over the slender curve of her thighs, lured by the siren call of their warm, smooth skin. Wove a path to the damp patch of fabric between them and, slipping his finger under the edge of her panties, found the hidden nub of flesh at her core.

She trembled and gave an inarticulate cry at the spasm that seized her. He touched her again, knowing well the exact spot that would give her the most pleasure. A subtle increase in pressure, a more urgent rhythm. Then the hiss of delicate silk giving way as he inserted three fingers between her and her underwear, the middle one sliding inside her dark wet confines at the same time that he relented and let his tongue dance with hers.

The sublime torture of having her tilt her hips backward in fluid compliance, and not take what she so willingly offered, almost killed him. The blood pounded through his veins, his lungs seized up, and how he didn't grind his teeth to dust was nothing short of miraculous. If she touched him, even fleetingly and even with the barrier of clothing depriving him of the intimacy he was affording her, he would explode. But she did not. His contained agony was eclipsed by her soft scream as she climaxed and collapsed against him, sobbing.

He held her until she grew calm again, then lifted her clear of his lap and deposited her back on the seat beside him.

"No," she begged, clinging to him. "Not until we both…together…please, Dario…!"

But he'd played a similar game of Russian roulette with her once before, and look where it had landed them. He wasn't going to make the same mistake again. "I didn't come prepared."

"What does it matter? You're my husband."

Oh, it mattered. It would continue to matter until they both knew without a shadow of doubt that he was the man she wanted, not just for a night, but forever.

Removing himself from further temptation, he stood up and stepped away from the swing. "This is hardly the time or the place, Maeve," he said. "Our absence has already been noticed. Antonia's serving dinner, and if we don't show up fast, she'll be sending someone to come looking for us."

She let out a horrified little yelp. "I hope you're joking."

"See for yourself."

She peeked around the side of the canopy, which had so effectively camouflaged them from view. The housekeeper, having set out the first course, was casting a searching glance around the empty terrace.

"Well, do something, for heaven's sake," Maeve whimpered, running agitated fingers through her hair. "I'm a mess. I can't have anyone see me looking like this."

No more could he. He might be talking good sense, but his body wasn't listening. He ached so viciously, he'd have plunged fully dressed into the pool, except it would only draw more attention to a situation he never should have allowed to get so far out of hand to begin with. "I'll go ahead and distract her," he said, collecting the champagne flutes and steadfastly willing his rebellious nether regions to behave. "Slip through the library to get back to your room, and join me when you're ready."

Regaining the sanctuary of her suite undetected, Maeve locked herself in the bathroom and, almost as baffled as she was ashamed, regarded herself in the full-length mirror. Her face was flushed, her lip gloss smeared, and her eyes glittered like demented beacons.

What in the world had come over her? Planning to seduce her husband was one thing, but attempting to do so where they might have been discovered ranked right up there with deciding to swim naked in broad daylight. Both were completely out of character, which gave rise to some disturbing questions.

Had she undergone a major personality change as a result of her head injury, and was that why Dario had so firmly resisted her? Was she proving to be as much of a stranger to him as he was to her? Or was it simply, as he'd tried to tell her before, that she was pushing too hard and too fast to find her way back to him?

One thing she did know. Whether or not he admitted it, he wanted her as ardently as she wanted him. He'd implied that their marriage hadn't been all smooth sailing before the accident, but regardless of what had transpired in the past, the sexual attraction between them had survived intact. Why, then, was he so unwilling to give in to it?

She had no answers but, as she freshened up and made herself presentable again, she determined she wouldn't rest until she found some. Since her husband was so unwilling to provide them and she'd rather eat worms than ask anything of her mother-in-law, she'd rely on her own ingenuity to put together the missing pieces that comprised the jigsaw puzzle of her life. That those answers existed, just a breath out of reach, had been made evident by the brief flash of memory that had assailed her earlier in the evening.

Her opportunity to do some sleuthing came the next day, when Dario left for Milan. Or, more accurately, the next night.

To make sure she didn't trip over the ever-vigilant Antonia or one of her minions, Maeve waited until after midnight before stealing out of her suite. Her first stop was his study, a room far enough removed from the staff quarters that she was in no danger of alerting anyone to her activities.

Although his desk was littered with the kind of paperwork one would expect of any corporate executive operating out of his home, there was absolutely nothing personal among it that she could see from her cursory investigation. None of the drawers were locked, which suggested they, too, were devoid of anything that might spark a memory, nor did the bookshelves yield any clues. Which left the computer. But even she, desperate though she was to reclaim her past, drew the line at going quite that far. Coming across something that happened to be lying out more or less in full view was one thing; violating his privacy by snooping through his files or e-mail, quite another.

Leaving the study exactly as she'd found it, she crept past the library and the media room, the big formal dining room and the elegant day salon. A few yards farther on, a set of tall double doors blocked her progress, but they opened at her touch and, as she'd suspected, marked the entrance to the master suite.

Like hers, it formed an arm of the villa's E-shaped floor plan. Unlike hers, it didn't share the space with two other suites, but occupied the entire wing.

When she touched the electric switch to her left, four wall sconces shed subdued light on a foyer that was almost as spacious as her living room in Vancouver. Oyster-white walls contrasted sharply with a jewel-toned Turkish area rug covering part of the black marble floor. Equally eye-catching were the vibrant colors of a bird-of-paradise bouquet on a table set against one wall. Two doors took up most of the third wall, with an arched opening leading to a sitting room filling the fourth.

She chose to explore the sitting area first. Tastefully furnished with sofas upholstered in crisp black-and-white-striped linen, the usual complement of occasional tables, strategically placed lamps, a sound system and a small ladies' writing desk, the room's most striking feature was the wall of floor-to-ceiling windows. They offered an unsurpassed view across the moonlit sea and gave access to yet another private pool and terrace furnished with table, chairs and sun lounges.

What struck her most forcibly, though, was the complete lack of personal touches within the room. No objets d'art or magazines littered the surface of the tables. No framed photographs graced the walls. No evidence at all, in fact, that anyone had ever actually used the place. Even the writing desk, which might reasonably be expected to contain some item of interest, revealed nothing but a couple of silver pens, a stack of embossed stationery and a small English-Italian dictionary.

Hoping for better luck elsewhere, she returned to the foyer and opened the first door on her left. A short hall led to the master bedroom, which, decorated chiefly in restful shades of misty blue-gray and white, made her ache for all the nights she'd not shared it with her husband.

Filmy draperies hung at the sliding glass doors that gave access to the pool and terrace. White fur rugs were scattered over the floor. In one corner, a potted tibouchina covered with purple blossoms stood beside a Victorian chaise longue upholstered in a soft gray toile depicting exotic birds. On the other side, a tulip-shaped Art Deco reading lamp fashioned from opaque glass stood on a little carved table, with just enough room next to it for a book and maybe a cup of hot chocolate.

In the opposite corner, a black iron floor candelabra shaped like a tree made a bold fashion statement, even though it lacked candles. The other source of light came from black-shaded lamps with heavy brass bases on the nightstands.

And then there was the most dominant feature of the room, the bed itself. Sumptuously proportioned and extravagantly dressed in the finest linens, it brought to mind images so stirring and erotic, Maeve's stomach turned over in a rolling somersault. Her mind might not remember writhing in ecstasy as she and Dario made love on its thick mattress, but her body certainly did.

Double en suite bath and dressing rooms opened off this room. Body lotions, bath oils and hand-milled soaps, as well as thick velvet towels monogrammed with her initials were meticulously set out in her bathroom. Those clothes not in her temporary quarters were arranged by color in the closets, along with shoes, wide-brimmed hats and other accessories.

But as with the bed and sitting rooms, they struck not a single chord of memory. And to add to the mystery of her past, a second door leading from the bedroom and connecting to who knew what, was locked, as was its counterpart in the foyer.

Disappointed, she retraced her steps throughout the entire suite. Everything was undeniably attractive, but the most important element, the one that made it home, was missing. It was all too eerily immaculate; a residence-in-waiting from which every conceivable flaw had been carefully erased. No trace of human trial and error or interaction remained. Whatever imperfections made up its past had been removed.

And she knew where they were hidden. Behind those locked doors.

Well, at least she'd narrowed down her search. Now all she had to do was find the missing key. But where to look? The most obvious places had turned up nothing. Probably Dario had a safe hidden somewhere, but even if she found it, without knowing the code to open it, she'd be no further ahead.

No, her only recourse lay with her husband. He was the real repository of her history, and one way or another she had to persuade him to share it with her.

As promised, he returned from Milan just in time to shower and change before dinner the following evening. As always, he looked divine in slim-fitting charcoal-gray trousers and a pearl-colored shirt against which his skin glowed like polished copper.

"You seem weary, Maeve," he commented, holding her at arm's length and inspecting her critically when he joined her. "There are dark smudges under your pretty eyes."

Guilt welled up in her. Of course she looked weary! For a start, duplicity didn't sit well with her. Add to that snooping through the house, then mulling over what might be behind those locked doors, and she'd managed only about four hours of sleep last night. "I missed you," she said. That much at least was no lie.

He traced his finger over her mouth. "Did you?"

"Yes," she quavered, finding his touch so wildly exciting that it was all she could do to breathe. "The villa isn't the same when you're not here. I hope you're not planning on going away again anytime soon."

"As a matter of fact, yes, I am. Tomorrow, in fact, to spend the weekend in Tunisia."

All the lovely warm sensations he so easily aroused vanished as if he'd flung cold water in her face. Not bothering to hide her disappointment, she said, "A man in your lofty position having to work on the weekend? Can't you send someone else in your place?"

"I wouldn't dream of it," he replied, filling their champagne flutes from the bottle of Cristal chilling in the wine bucket. "This trip will be strictly for pleasure."

"I see. Well, I hope you have a very lovely time." She tilted her chin, praying for pride to conceal her hurt, and took an inelegant but fortifying swig of champagne.

"And *I* hope," he continued, amusement silvering his voice at her conspicuously acidic response, "that you'll come with me."

She choked as her next mouthful went down the wrong way. Had she heard him correctly? "Go with you?" she spluttered.

"Provided you feel up to it, of course. If not, we'll forget the whole idea."

She swallowed an unseemly hiccup. "Surely a more pertinent question is, are you quite sure *you're* up to it?"

"Well, who else would I take? You are my wife, after all."

"I know. It's one of the few things I *am* aware of."

"Then why the hesitation? I thought you'd welcome a change of scene."

"I would," she agreed. "It's your about-face that's giving me pause. Or is your memory as faulty as mine and you've forgotten that, as recently as two days ago, you insisted I'm not yet well enough to face the outside world?"

"I've forgotten nothing, but you've made so little progress since you came home that I'm no longer sure keeping you secluded is helping your recovery. Perhaps, instead of trying to revive old memories, we should concentrate on forging new ones, and where better to begin than in a place you've never been before?" He looked at her expectantly. "Well? What do you think?"

She lifted her shoulders, bemused. "I hardly know what to say."

"Say yes. Let's start over and see where it leads us."

"A second honeymoon, you mean?"

"*Sì.*"

"As in you and I…um…you know…?"

"Precisely. Starting tonight. It's either that, or I enter a monastery, because keeping my distance from you is having a most deleterious effect on my health, not to mention my sanity."

"Is it really?" For the life of her, she couldn't quite contain her delight. "My goodness, I'd never have guessed."

Laughing, he reached across the table and grasped her hands. "You certainly would, you little minx. You know exactly the effect you have on me."

"But I never thought you'd give in to it."

"Don't underestimate your power, Maeve. I have missed holding you close while you sleep, missed waking up next to you each morning, and deeply missed making love with you. But not furtively or hastily, as almost happened the other night, which is why, before I left for Milan, I instructed Antonia to prepare our private rooms for your return."

Resuming her married life was what she'd wanted almost from day one, but now that it lay within her grasp, some of its luster faded. She'd been right in thinking the master wing looked naked under all its chic finery. It had indeed been swept clean. The secrets of the past were not about to be revealed, after all, merely shoved out of sight. And she'd bet her last dollar they were securely under lock and key in that other room.

That a deafening hush had descended over the terrace became apparent when Dario said, "I hoped for a more enthusiastic response, *mio dolce*."

"This is all so unexpected, I'm still trying to take it in," she said, to cover up the suspicions racing around in her head. "I suppose, if I'm really honest, I half expect you to change your mind again."

Coming to where she sat, he pulled her to her feet, extracted a small leather pouch from his shirt pocket and tipped the contents onto the table. A pair of white-gold wedding bands rolled over the polished surface and came to rest at the base of her wineglass. Taking her left hand, he slipped the smaller of the two on the third finger. "Once again, Maeve Montgomery, I take you for my lawful wife. Is that enough to reassure you?"

The ring, though a little loose fitting, gleamed in the candlelight and felt so deliciously right that for the moment only one thing mattered. She picked up the other ring, slid it on his finger. "And I once again take you, Dario Costanzo, to be my husband."

He handed her her wineglass and raised his in a toast. "Then here's to us, *mia bella*."

"To us."

The intensity of his gaze as they sipped made her blush. "I do believe," he murmured hoarsely, setting both flutes back on the table and reaching for her, "that it's customary at this point for the groom to kiss his bride."

Struggling to breathe normally, she nodded. "I do believe you're right."

He cupped her face between his palms and lowered his head.

Brushed his lips over hers lightly, fleetingly, then with crushing urgency, as one hand stroked past her shoulders to settle intimately at her waist. "After which," he said, lifting his head to gaze deep into her eyes, "comes the first dance."

Slowly he clasped his other hand with hers and guided her across the terrace. They moved together effortlessly, his longer legs accommodating her shorter steps, his lips skimming her temples.

A clock inside the villa rang out the hour, nine musical chimes that briefly drowned out a silken-voiced tenor crooning softly from stereo speakers mounted on the outside wall, then drifted out into the night.

Caught in a sudden powerful tide of déjà vu, Maeve yearned toward her husband. Once before he had held her in his arms, and a chime had echoed across the quiet sea. As the bell-like tone died away, he'd kissed her just so, under the same stars that sprinkled the heavens now. And it had been wonderful. Magical. She knew it as surely as she knew her own name.

"I remember," she breathed. "Dario, it's all coming back to me."

CHAPTER EIGHT

"ALL what?"

"Kissing you like this. Dancing with you under the stars."

"Nothing unusual in that." In marked contrast to her excitement, Dario kept his response determinedly casual. "It's the sort of thing married couples do all the time."

Except that, in their case, it had happened only once before, the night he'd seduced her. Considering the aftermath, he'd as soon it didn't all come rushing back in vivid Technicolor now. They wouldn't stand much chance of starting over if she recalled the embarrassment and hurt she'd suffered at his hands, the day after she'd surrendered her virginity to him. And in his opinion, a fresh start was long overdue.

He was tired of fighting his feelings for her, and of living like a monk despite being tempted beyond human endurance. Among other considerations, walking around with a permanent erection was humiliating, as he'd discovered during his meetings in Milan when his thoughts had repeatedly strayed from the serious business of international finance, to the much more pleasurable contemplation of soon making love to his wife.

Maeve wasn't helping matters, either, in looking more desirable by the day. Plenty of homemade pasta, good, fresh seafood washed down with excellent local wine, and the *mostazzoli panteschi* and other pastries she enjoyed so much had eliminated her gaunt angles and restored her delicious curves. Add to that her impeccable sense of style, and he'd have had to be both neutered and brain dead not to desire her.

Plainly put, he missed the wife he'd grown to love, and not just because of the sex or lack thereof. He missed her companionship, her sharp intelligence and her quick wit. He missed how they would lock glances across a roomful of people at a dreary corporate party, and smile in complicit understanding that they'd enjoy their own private celebration at the first opportunity. Yet he'd been forced to keep his distance from her because he didn't trust himself to be close.

Even worse, Maeve hadn't seen their son in nearly nine weeks. The longer the separation continued, the harder it would be on everyone. Already she'd missed so much of their child's development; milestones that would never be repeated. Sebastiano had three teeth now, which was three more than he'd had the last time she'd seen him. He pretty much sat up unaided, and already was trying to crawl by pulling himself over the floor like a baby seal. He gurgled with pleasure every time he saw his little cousin, Cristina, and had bonded with his aunt to the point that he'd cried and reached out for her the last time Dario had tried to pick him up. Tearing him away from the people who'd become his primary family was going to be painful for everyone involved.

That Dario was hugely indebted to Giuliana and her husband, Lorenzo, for helping out by taking the baby into their household and into their hearts, went without saying. But the boy should be riding around on his own father's shoulders and sleeping in his own crib, with his own mother singing him to sleep at night.

Dario had had enough of feeling more like a visitor than a parent, and more than enough of paying discreet visits to his sister's, in order to spend a stolen hour or two with his son. It irked him to be put in such a position. No man should have to sneak around to see his own child.

But Peruzzi's warnings had left their mark. Dario had no way of knowing how Maeve would react when her memory returned, but he did know he wouldn't be responsible for causing her more grief than she'd already have to face. Whether Yves Gauthier had been friend or lover scarcely counted for much, compared to her having wiped all knowledge of her son from her mind.

Nor was that all. As her husband, Dario was beyond weary of the half-truths and evasions he was feeding his wife. He didn't handle well not being in control, and if it were up to him, he'd tell her everything, sort out the mess they'd found themselves in and go forward from there. In light of Peruzzi's warnings, however, it was a risk he dared not take.

Unaware of the direction his thoughts had gone, Maeve sagged against him now. "You believe I'm grasping at straws, don't you?"

"Not necessarily," he said, "but if you're determined to immortalize a particular night, why not let this be the one?"

"You're right." Drifting back to the table, she sat down and toyed with the cook's very excellent *linguine allo scoglia*, mounds of clams, prawns, shrimp and mussels bathed in a rich tomato sauce. "Tell me more about our trip tomorrow. Exactly where are we going in Tunisia?"

"The capital itself, Tunis. It's an interesting city that I think you'll enjoy."

She nibbled a fat prawn thoughtfully. "What should I pack in the way of clothes?"

"For the evening, one of your pretty dinner dresses. During the day, something in cool cotton, a couple of wide-brimmed hats, comfortable flat-heeled sandals and sunscreen," he said, tackling his own meal. "Walking's the only way to appreciate everything the city has to offer, and it's going to be hot. Oh, and fairly modest clothes—I won't stand for strange men burping at you."

"Burping?" She choked back a laugh. "No wonder you call them strange!"

"That's not why. Burping's the Tunisian way of showing appreciation for a pretty woman, and since most local women cover themselves from head to toe in public, tourists are fair game for any man with a roving eye."

"If I didn't know better, I'd think you were jealous."

"Perhaps I have reason to be," he said, an unexpectedly bitter note coating his reply.

"What?" She stared at him, shocked.

Cursing himself—the festering accusation was out before he could contain it, and hardly an auspicious way to effect the kind of reconciliation he was hoping for—he added swiftly, "It's the price every husband pays for having a beautiful wife, Maeve."

"Well, let me put this particular husband's mind at rest," she said flatly. "I don't care how many men burp at me, I only have eyes for you."

There it was again, the erection that never slept! "How hungry are you?" he inquired huskily.

"For this?" She poked her fork around in the unquestionably delicious food remaining on her plate. "Not very."

No more was he. "Then what do you say to our continuing this conversation someplace more private?"

"I think it's the best idea you've had in ages."

Earlier, Antonia or one of the maids had added a few more romantic touches to the master suite. A bouquet of lilies filled the sitting area with fragrance. In the bedroom, a single rose in a bud vase stood on the little table next to the Victorian chaise longue. More than a dozen squat candles in glass cups suspended from the tree-shaped floor candelabra cast a glimmering light over the bed, but left the corners of the room swathed in moon-shot darkness.

All this Maeve took in with what she hoped showed just the right degree of curiosity. But despite her best efforts, her gaze repeatedly wandered to the locked doors, first the one in the foyer, and then the other, there in the bedroom.

That Dario noticed quickly became apparent. "It doesn't matter that you don't recognize anything," he said, rather firmly steering her away from the room at large, and through the open glass doors to the terrace. "Tonight's about us and the future, *tesoro*."

Outside, more candles burned in faceted glass hurricane lamps set around the pool, and waiting on the table was an ice bucket containing another bottle of champagne and two long-stemmed frosted glasses. As the perfect introduction to a night of seduction, she could hardly have asked for better.

Yet her delight was tainted by something far less pleasant. "It's not that, exactly," she muttered, treading a fine line between truth and lie.

"Nor is it about rushing to make love before you're ready," he assured her. "We take this at your pace, Maeve. I wouldn't have it any other way."

It wasn't that, either. The simple fact was, she was riddled with guilt. If only she'd known this was how the evening would end, she'd never have come sneaking through the suite, the night before.

A good marriage should be based on trust and respect, so what did it say about theirs, that she'd behaved so shabbily? Yet to admit to her transgression now was more than she could bring herself to do. After all, it wasn't as if she'd discovered anything significant, or tried to pick the locks on the doors to that other room.

But that line of reasoning offered cold comfort and prompted her to say, "That's not what's bothering me, Dario. It's my conscience. You've been so patient with me ever since I came home, but I've been a pretty poor wife, and I'm sorry for that."

"You're here now, and that's all I ask for," Dario almost purred, drawing her down to sit on his lap. "Do you have any idea, *innamorata,* how empty these rooms have been without you, or how long the nights that you have not shared our bed?"

If he never did anything more than speak to her like that, with his voice resonating over her nerve endings until her entire being hummed with awareness, she could die a happy woman.

He mesmerized her. Rescued her from the mundane and, with a fleeting kiss here, a featherlight touch there, transported her to a world far removed from the ordinary.

He shaped her mouth with his thumb, a tactile benediction so exquisite that she quivered uncontrollably. Stroked his fingertip the length of her arm, from her wrist to her shoulder, imbuing the caress with a tenderness that made her want to weep. He traced the line of her collarbone, the contour of her throat, and left her gasping for more. Did all with such consummate finesse that she was hardly aware of when they returned to the intimacy of the bedroom, or how it was that they were standing naked before each other.

As though seeing her for the first time, he held her at arm's length and let his eyes roam from her breasts to the indentation of her waist, then past the curve of her hips to the shadowed juncture of her thighs. And every place his gaze touched caught fire until she was burning all over.

"I thought I remembered how lovely you are," he finally murmured in hushed tones, "but would you believe I did not do you justice?"

"Yes," she said on a breathless sigh, raging desire giving her the courage to scrutinize him with the same minute attention to every detail of his physique that he had afforded to hers. "Memory so often plays us false."

The candle flames bathed his olive skin in tongues of shimmering light. They played over his torso, illuminating the muscled slope of his shoulders, the breadth of his chest, the hard, flat plane of his midriff, and the long, strong length of his legs. They showcased the urgent thrust of his erection that told her more plainly than anything words could convey how much he desired her.

The day over a week ago that she'd stepped out of his private jet and seen him for what, as far as she was concerned, was the first time, she'd thought him the most handsome man she'd ever met. But only now did she appreciate the extent of his masculine beauty. He stood before her like a god hammered from bronze and dusted with gold. Proud, powerful, invincible.

He left her weak with longing; dazed with wonder. "Dario?" she whispered.

"I'm here, and I'm yours," he said, the timbre of his voice chasing new thrills over her skin. "Show me what you want, *amore mio,* and I will give it to you."

Hypnotized by his unwavering stare, she put her hand to his chest. Felt the strong, steady beat of his heart. Circled his flat nipple with her forefinger. "I want you all of you," she told him and, with new daring, slid her hand past his waist and flexed her fingers possessively around his erection. How smooth and heavy it was. Soft as silk, strong as steel.

"I want to feel you hard against me and hear your breath catch in your throat," she whispered, her words vibrating with suppressed passion. "I want you to take me to bed and fill me so that there are no empty corners left where I can hide."

With a muffled groan, he swung her into his arms. The mattress sighed as he lowered her to it and lay down beside her.

Stirred by the night wind, the filmy drapes at the open glass doors whispered applause. The candlelight winked.

As though he'd been waiting permission from all three, he finally kissed her. Deeply, hungrily. And when that wasn't enough to satisfy either of them, he put his mouth in other places, scorching a path from her breasts to her navel, and lower still to her thighs. Boldly, he flicked his tongue between them, searing their tender skin and inching them apart.

Momentarily shocked, she stiffened. But he'd done more than inch her legs apart. He'd forced open a chink in her memory of other such times. Times her body recalled with aching intensity, even if clouds continued to swirl in her mind.

He had done this before. *They* had done this before, with her clawing at his shoulders as she writhed before the onrushing waves of ecstasy threatening to drown her. And with him holding her hips captive so that she could not escape the pleasure he was so determined to give to her.

Tension caught her in an unforgiving spiral. Wound tighter and tighter. So tight that perspiration dimmed her vision. A silent scream rose in her throat, but before it could find voice, she soared, exploding into a hundred thousand prisms of light, each more blinding than its predecessor.

Desperate to anchor herself to earth, to him, she cried his name. He heard her unspoken plea and, bracing himself on his forearms, he lowered himself until his flesh was touching hers, there where she craved him the most.

Smoothly he filled her. Carried her in a rhythm at first slow and easy and so deeply intimate that her eyes flooded with tears. Then, as the momentum built, a different kind of emotion swept over her, one laced with greed because a little wasn't enough. She wanted everything he had to give her. She wanted his soul in exchange for the one he'd taken from her.

But she should have known that nothing worth having ever came without a price. As she took from him, so he robbed her a second time. Even as he groaned and shuddered in release, her world splintered again with such unrestrained abandon, she thought her heart would burst.

He collapsed on top of her, his chest heaving. The thudding silence that followed roared through her mind like a tornado. If this was how it had been between them before, drenched in glorious passion, how could she not have remembered, and why had he hinted that all was not well in their marriage?

Yesterday she thought finding the answers would dispel the sense of doom haunting her. Now she wasn't sure she wanted to tamper with perfection. Better to do as he suggested: leave the past behind and carve a new path into the future.

Stirring, he lifted his head and stared down at her, his eyes smoldering in the subdued light. "Did I please you, *tesoro?*"

"Oh, you pleased me," she said. "You pleased me very much. I have not felt so complete in a very long time."

The dark shadow forever looming over her had lifted somewhat, and for the first time in weeks she slept deeply, dreamlessly, safe in her husband's arms.

They left early the next morning, shortly after sunrise, which put paid to any idea she'd harbored of a more intimate start to the day. Dario was all business as he'd shooed her out of bed and into the bathroom.

"Ordinarily I'd have taken you by boat," he explained, during the short drive to the airport at the north end of the island, "but Tunis is a fascinating city and with only two days in which to show it to you, I've saved us some time by chartering a private aircraft. We'll be there in time for breakfast."

A perfectly logical explanation, at least on the surface, but she was convinced there was another reason he was so anxious to vacate the villa.

"Storage," he'd informed her tersely when, in the course

of getting ready to leave, she'd inquired ever so casually what lay behind the locked doors in their suite.

"Storage for what?"

"Just stuff," he replied, and practically strong-armed her out of the house and into the Porsche.

He was lying. She knew it as surely as she knew her own name. But she could hardly call him on it since she wasn't entirely without guile herself.

By nine o'clock they were seated at a sidewalk café on the Avenue Habib Bouguiba, breakfasting on peaches, figs, oven-warm brioches spread with quince jam, and rich, flavorful coffee. The slight tension that had marked their departure from Pantelleria melted in the North African sun, and Dario was again the ideal husband from last night, trapping her knee between both of his under the table, hypnotizing her with his smile and devouring her in his sultry gaze.

Afterward, they strolled hand in hand past old bookstores, galleries and flower stands to the Cathedral of St. Vincent-de-Paul, and stood in awe before its impressive neo-Romanesque facade. An excellent tour guide, Dario explained that in addition to containing the tomb of the Unknown Soldier, the cathedral was also the largest surviving building from the French Colonial era.

From there they entered the Medina, the medieval Muslim town situated only a stone's throw away from the Christian church, yet a world removed from the bustling modern city beyond its gateway. Graceful minarets rose up white and dazzling against the deep-blue sky. Ancient palaces and mosques vied for space with crowded souks selling everything from spices to clothing, perfume to jewelry. Pottery, brass and carpets spilled out of tiny shops into the street.

Men wearing flowers in their hair infused the morning with the fragrance of jasmine that vied with cloves and incense to permeate the air. Merchants bargained in Arabic and a smattering of French, English, Italian and German with tourists looking to take home souvenirs. Barbers plied their trade on every corner.

Maeve was enchanted by it all: the scents, the sounds, the atmosphere, the exotic foreignness. Nothing here hinted at a troubled past. No disapproving mother-in-law lurked nearby. No secrets were hidden behind locked doors. She was happy and in love, and for as long as it lasted, she intended to savor every second.

"I'm so glad to be here with you," she told Dario, when they stopped midmorning to refresh themselves with tiny cups of sweetened mint tea.

"And I with you." He touched her hand, tracing his finger over her wedding ring. "I must have been mad to wait so long to claim you as my wife again."

His words filled her heart to overflowing.

They resumed their explorations, wending their way through the maze of street to Ez Zitouna, the Mosque of the Olive Tree. Here the gold souks and other so-called "clean" professions stood closest to the walls, while the "unclean" professions such as dyeing and crude metal work were farther away.

It was a shopper's paradise and Maeve was fascinated by the delicate silver jewelry, sequined and embroidered accessories, and finely woven wool which only the very wealthy could afford.

"Some of my former clients would kill to own this," she remarked, examining a beautiful fringed shawl in vibrant shades of blue and crimson.

"But it was designed with you in mind," Dario said, and over her objections promptly started bargaining with the merchant to acquire it for her.

When they finally left the Medina around three o'clock, he'd also bought her an exquisite antique perfume bottle and a bird cage intricately carved from white wood, "because," he insisted, "no wife of mine is leaving here without something to remind her of her second honeymoon."

"But I don't own a bird," she protested, laughing as he juggled the cage through the crowds.

Unfazed, he said, "I'm sure they sell those, as well. We'll come back tomorrow and look for one."

The driver he'd hired to pick them up at the airport had dropped off their luggage at the place they were staying. A French Colonial mansion converted to a small boutique hotel, it was exclusive, elegant and charming. Their suite, overlooking the rear gardens and the Mediterranean, was shielded from the city noise and cooled by ceiling fans. The floors were marble; the furniture, antique provincial; the wall hangings, silk.

By then, worn-out from the early start to the day and the heat, Maeve was glad to kick off her sandals, shed her dress for a cotton robe and stretch out on the bed for a late-afternoon nap. But that plan went awry when Dario, who'd gone out to the terrace to make a phone call, came back into the room.

She felt the mattress give under his weight, then his lips were on hers, his kisses sliding from soft and persuasive to hard and commanding.

Love in the afternoon, she discovered, had much to recommend it. Leisurely, splashed with sunshine, it invited a different kind of intimacy from that of the night before; a more acute visual scrutiny than candle flame and moonlight allowed.

She saw his mouth curve with pleasure when her nipples peaked under his grazing caress, and the slow, sultry sweep of his lashes as he buried himself deep inside her. She watched the passion flare in his eyes, the sweat beading his brow and the hard line of his clenched jaw as he fought the tide threatening to overpower him.

Clutching his shoulders and rising to meet him as her own body answered the demands of his, she glimpsed the reflection of their tangled limbs in the gilt-framed mirror hanging above the dresser on the opposite wall, his burnished by the Mediterranean sun to the color of brown sugar against her paler skin tones. Even as her eyes closed in surrender, his taut buttocks, the sensual rhythm of his hips, the flexing and contracting of his back muscles, imprinted themselves forever in her mind.

Drowsy and sated, with the damp heat of utter gratification still binding her to him, she kissed his throat and whispered, "Nothing that happened in the past matters to me any longer, Dario. From now on, this day, this moment are all I care about, and all I need on which to build our future."

Somehow she'd said the wrong thing. Although he didn't move a muscle, sudden distance sprang up between them, induced by a tension so potent that it filled the entire room. "I wish it were that simple, my darling wife," he said. "Unfortunately, it isn't."

CHAPTER NINE

"I THOUGHT," she said in a small, crushed voice, "that's what you wanted."

More fool him, he'd thought so, too. But that, Dario realized grimly, was what happened when a man let his carnal appetite get the better of his judgment. He rationalized every decision he arrived at, even when none made sense. The truth was, there was no escaping the past and there never would be.

"What I want," he said carefully, "is to put the past behind us. That's not quite the same thing as pretending it never happened. Our history—what we've done, where we've been, who we've known—makes us who we are today, Maeve."

"What if we find we don't like who we are?"

"Then we make changes and try to put right the things that went wrong. We don't lop off an arm or leg because it hurts, and we can't just cut out a chunk of our past if we happen not to like it."

"Then why did you bring me here?"

He propped himself on one elbow and looked down at her. Her face remained flushed from lovemaking, but the light in her beautiful blue eyes was bruised with pain. "Because I see you struggling to regain your focus, and I hoped a new scene, new faces, might help. And because I'm a selfish bastard who wanted you all to myself for a couple of days."

"I wanted that, as well." She sighed tremulously. "I wish we could stay here. I wish we never had to go back to Pantelleria."

"Can you tell me what it is about the place that disturbs you so?"

"I feel too…confined. My entire life has narrowed to what lies within the walls of the villa, and it's suffocating me."

It hadn't always been like that, but for her own sake, it had to be that way now. There wasn't a soul on the island who hadn't heard about the accident and the circumstances surrounding it. It had been all anyone had talked about for weeks. Left to roam about at will as she once had, she'd be recognized and, if there was a greater risk than his telling her all that had come to pass, it was having her hear it from someone else.

"There's something about the place that haunts me," she went on, with a tiny, helpless shudder. "It's as if something dark and fearful is lurking in the corner, waiting to jump out and destroy me. I wish, if you know what it is, that you'd just tell me."

"It might be that we argued and said some hurtful things to each other, the last time we were together before the accident."

"What kind of things?"

"Outside commitments. My obligations as a businessman and a husband, yours as my wife. Loyalties, priorities, casting blame, and misunderstandings in general." He shrugged. "It's not something I'm very proud to look back on."

She regarded him in sudden hope. "Is that how the car crash

came about—we argued, I got upset and drove off, and you're afraid I'll blame you for letting me go when I was in no fit state to drive?"

He wished he'd kept his mouth shut because, at this rate, she'd stumble on the truth before much longer, and he wasn't sure he'd know how to handle the fallout. "No. I wasn't on the island the day that happened. I was in Milan."

"Oh," she said thoughtfully. "Then who was driving?"

Dio, the one question he'd hoped to avoid! "A summer visitor who'd rented a nearby villa for a few weeks. I can't tell you much more than that."

"But—"

Loath to continue a subject painfully fraught with conjecture, he took her hand and urged it down his belly to cradle him, knowing her touch was all it would take to make him hard again. "But nothing, *amore mio!*" he muttered against her mouth, tormenting her in deliberate seduction exactly as she was tormenting him, because it was the only way he could think of to silence her questions. "Why are we talking about other people, when a second honeymoon should be only about a man and his bride?"

She responded as he'd hoped she would. "I don't know," she gasped, her eyes glazing with pleasure as he found the erogenous spot between her legs.

He stroked her until she came, and when at last he took her completely, burying himself deep in her soft, welcoming depths, it was with something approaching desperation, as if by doing so he might bury his own doubts, as well as hers.

Because she wasn't the only one afraid that the truth might smash their newfound happiness into oblivion.

* * *

She must have drifted to sleep in his arms because when next she opened her eyes, darkness had fallen and Dario was gone, but a patch of light from the open bathroom door and the sound of running water told her where she might find him.

With a boldness that would have shocked her a week ago, she went to join him. A towel slung around his hips, he stood before one of the two hand-painted wash bowls, scraping a razor over his soap-lathered jaw. Drops of water glinted in his thick hair and sparkled on his shoulders.

"*Ciao,* sleepyhead," he crooned, inspecting her naked body with such unabashed appreciation that she blushed from head to toe. "*Venire qui e darmi un bacio.* Come and give me a kiss."

"Not a chance," she squealed, ducking away as he advanced on her with the clear intention of smearing shaving soap all over as much of her as he could reach.

He was quicker though, and cornered her in the big double shower stall. In the ensuing scuffle, his towel slipped its anchor and fell off. Feigning dismay at the sight of his virile proportions, she shielded her eyes. "Oh, dear! I didn't mean to have *that* kind of effect on you."

Laughing, he pinned her against the tiled wall and turned on the cold water, full force. "Sure you did, *la mia principessa nuda,* and now you'll have to pay the price."

"Stop!" she shrieked, goose bumps the size of raisins puckering her skin under the chilly blast. "There has to be a more humane way to resolve the issue that's…um, arisen between us."

"In fact there is, and believe me I'd resort to it in a flash if I hadn't made a dinner reservation that leaves us only half an hour to dress and get to the restaurant." He slapped her playfully on the bottom. "So hop to it, honey, as they say in your country, and we'll resume this discussion later."

The dinner dress she'd brought with her was one she'd come across by accident, stashed at the back of her closet behind all the others, many of them still too large for her. Long and black, with a narrow skirt and silver embroidery along the neckline and at the hem, it was chic and elegant without being overly formal. A gauzy wrap spattered with tiny silver stars, silver sandals and matching clutch purse, and white-gold hoop earrings completed the ensemble, and from Dario's low, drawn-out whistle when he saw her, she'd chosen well.

He took her to a wonderful restaurant in the very heart of the Medina. Hundreds of years old, it oozed pure exotic atmosphere with its flowing draperies, brass oil lamps, and pointed arches fronted by gilt lattices reminiscent of the kind seen in old Hollywood spy movies.

Taking off their shoes, they sat on rush matting on a raised platform and dined on fresh Mediterranean lobster and succulent lamb flavored with coriander and saffron, accompanied by traditional couscous and a fine local wine. This last surprised Maeve, not just because of its quality, but that it was available at all.

"Alcohol's allowed because Islamic law isn't adhered to quite as rigidly in Tunisia as in other Muslim countries," Dario explained, when she commented. "Most restaurants serve wine, at least in the city, probably a leftover custom from French colonial times. How's your lamb, by the way?"

"Can't you tell?" She closed her eyes in pure enjoyment.

She'd been too hot to eat much during the day and was starving. "It's delectable, and so is the lobster."

"Make sure you leave room for dessert. They have first-rate honey cakes stuffed with dates on the menu, as well as honey and almonds in layers of pastry like Greek baklava, except they call it baklawa here. With your sweet tooth, you'll probably want to try some of both."

"You seem to know the place pretty well. Do I take it this isn't your first visit?"

"I've been here a time or two, yes," he admitted. "Back in my wild bachelor days, before I met you."

"Hmm." She pursed her lips and looked teasingly at him from the corner of her eye. "I don't think I want to know about that."

"There's nothing much to tell. Being here now with you is far more memorable."

"For me, too. I'm enjoying myself so much, Dario."

He lifted her hand to his lips and kissed her fingertips. "Then we'll come back another time, stay longer and ride camels in the Sahara."

"I'm not sure I'm ready for that. I've never even been on a horse."

"You've probably never tried belly dancing, either, but there's a first time for everything," he said, pointing to where a team of young women appeared from behind a curtain.

They began to weave their sinuous way across the floor, watched by men lounging against the walls and smoking hookah pipes. The music, provided by a quartet clad in bedouin robes, consisted of a sort of zither, a simple recorder, a small hand drum and a tambourine. Even to Maeve's untutored ear, the repetitive melody and persistent rhythm bore an unmistakably Arabic flavor.

The dancers wore wide, filmy pajama bottoms and bralike tops draped with gold-beaded fringes that shimmied with every undulation. In view of the amount of skin exposed between the two, how the bottoms stayed up and tops stayed on was nothing short of amazing.

Noting her absorbed interest in the spectacle, Dario said with an evil grin, "Would you like me to ask if they'll give you a lesson, my dear? I'm sure they'd be happy to oblige."

"Okay—if you'll try a hookah pipe."

"Sorry, I don't smoke."

"Then I don't shimmy," she said, and settled in the curve of his arm, content to watch the show, nibble baklawa, and sip Tunisian brandy made from figs and Turkish-style coffee served in tiny cups.

They left the restaurant slightly before eleven o'clock. Tunis after sundown was something of a surprise, she discovered. Instead of rushing around as they had during the day, people sat peacefully wherever they happened to find themselves, whether it be a park bench or their own doorstep, talking quietly as they recovered from the intense heat of the day.

Once back at the hotel, Maeve leaned against the wall of their suite's little terrace and gazed out at the nighttime view. Directly ahead, the dark mass of the sea rolled somnolently ashore. To her right, floodlit domes and minarets made up the city skyline. "This has been the experience of a lifetime, Dario," she told him, her senses alive with all she'd seen and heard and tasted. "I feel as if I'm living a scene from *One Thousand and One Nights*."

Standing behind her, he lowered the zipper on her dress slightly and pressed a hot, openmouthed kiss on her exposed shoulder. The tactile impact reverberated all the way to the soles of her feet.

"And this particular night isn't yet over. As I recall, we have unfinished business to attend to," he murmured. "Slip into something more comfortable, *mio dolce,* while I order us a bottle of champagne."

But she didn't need champagne to set the mood, any more than she needed the peignoir she'd so carefully included in her suitcase. The wine grew warm, the negligee spent the night on the floor in a heap of white lace, and Dario loved her with an inventiveness and passion that stole her breath away.

He explored every inch of her, cherishing her toes, her instep, the soft, sensitive skin at the back of her knees. He kissed her breasts, swirled his tongue at her navel, buried his mouth between her legs.

He made her tremble and shudder. And when she thought she'd slide into madness from the sheer exquisite ache of wanting, he'd sidle against her, then retreat before she could imprison him within the folds of her eager flesh.

When finally he took possession of her, she contracted around him in endless spasms of ecstasy that racked her body and left it glistening with sweat. But when at last he climaxed and took her with him yet again, it was glorious: a wild, delirious ride to the ends of the earth and back again.

Limp and spent, she collapsed in his arms, knowing that no matter what the future held, this was a night she would never forget.

* * *

She slept like a child, utterly relaxed, her body warm and soft, her breathing smooth and even. Her hair curled damply on her forehead. Her lashes lay thick against her cheek. Her hand curled trustingly on his chest.

Had he somehow effected a miracle? Dario wondered. Could a weekend of hot sex and romance mend a marriage that had grown progressively shakier with each passing month and culminated in a row that had almost cost her her life?

Unwilling to get down to specifics, he'd been deliberately vague when she'd asked what their last argument had been about, before the accident. But far from fading over time, the details remained sharp in his mind, stained with guilt and ugly suspicion.

It had started the first weekend in August when he came home from an unusually long business trip to Australia. The previous summer, after he'd brought Maeve to Italy as his bride, he'd explained that his work involved a lot of travel and they'd agreed it made sense for her to remain in the penthouse in Milan during his absences. His family was close by, and so was her obstetrician. After Sebastiano was born at the end of January, however, she began spending increasing time on Pantelleria, whether or not Dario was out of town.

"It's more relaxed here," she explained, when he asked her about it. "I'm under less social pressure and have more time to enjoy my baby. You're so busy during the week that we hardly see each other, anyway, but if you fly down on Friday evening and stay until Monday morning, we can at least be together then."

What she didn't say, but which he knew to be true, was that she wanted to escape his mother, who doted on her new grandson, but made no secret of her aversion to Maeve. "She's a spineless nobody who entrapped our son, and not the daughter-in-law I hoped for," he'd overheard Celeste remark to his father, during one of her periodic visits to corporate headquarters.

"You weren't the daughter-in-law my mother envisaged, either," his father had replied, "but she finally accepted you, and I suggest you learn from her example. Dario's his own man, just as I was. He's made his choice, and from everything I see, done not too badly for himself."

But in May and the onset of hotter weather, the entire Costanzo clan moved to their summer homes on Pantelleria. Like him, his father and brother-in-law spent the week in Milan and joined their families on the weekend, leaving the women to keep each other company the rest of the time. And that's when the rot really set in. Giuliana and Maeve had connected from the first and grown close as sisters. But his mother and Maeve were a whole other story, as Dario learned on his return from Australia.

Celeste wasted no time airing her grievances and cornered him in the garden his first day back. "She's inexperienced and should be grateful for my help," she complained, referring to a confrontation that had taken place a few days earlier to do with what she perceived to be Maeve's inept mothering skills. "I know what's best for my grandson."

"You need to take a step back and stop interfering," Dario informed her flatly. "And stop trying to undermine Maeve's self-confidence, as well, while you're at it."

"I'd have thought you'd appreciate my keeping an eye on her when you're not here," she retaliated. "All things considered."

He wasn't about to give her satisfaction by asking what *all things considered* amounted to. "She doesn't need anyone keeping an eye on her in my absence. I trust her judgment implicitly."

"A little too much, if you ask me," his mother said ambiguously, and when he responded by starting to walk away, stopped him short by bringing up the subject of Yves Gauthier, a man new to the island of whom Dario had previously been only vaguely aware.

"He's Canadian, just like her," Celeste continued scornfully, "and calls himself an artist, although not one any of us has ever heard of. He's leased the Belvisi place for the summer, but it's no secret that while you were away, he was seen more often at your home than his own. From all appearances, he and your wife have become, shall we say for want of a better description, very close *friends.*"

Still refusing to rise to the intended bait, Dario said, "Not surprising. They share a common background."

His mother sniffed disparagingly. "'Common' being the operative word."

"I'd have thought that by now you'd learned your lesson and knew better than to go around stirring up trouble where none exists," he told her sharply. "It didn't work when you tried it with Giuliana and Lorenzo, and it won't work now. Maeve is my wife and the mother of my son, and that's never going to change."

She lifted her shoulders in her signature elegant shrug. "If that's really what you want, then at least let me say this. It's just as well you're planning to take a break from the office and spend a week or two here because, whether or not you believe me, Yves Gauthier needs to be reminded of his proper place, and it is not making himself at home on your territory."

Dario had laughed, and accused her of letting her imagination run away with her, but the seed of doubt had been planted. He began to notice how frequently Maeve brought up Gauthier's name in conversation, and how the Canadian had insinuated himself into their tight social circle.

Dario had never been jealous of another man in his life. The women he'd dated in the past had never given him cause to be. That, as a husband, he found himself at the mercy of such demeaning weakness now both shamed and infuriated him.

Determined not to let it gain the upper hand, he did his best to stamp it out, but it got the better of him just three days into his supposed vacation time, when he and his parents were recalled to the head office for an emergency meeting of the board of directors. Giuliana and Lorenzo, the other two involved, were visiting friends in Paris and flew directly from there to Milan.

"But you only just got home," Maeve complained, when she heard. "Can't they manage without you, for once?"

"Not this time," he said. "We've run into a major snag with an overseas operation that could cost us millions."

"But we never get any alone time anymore."

He forbore to point out that was as much by her choice as his, and said reasonably, "Come with me for a change. Show Sebastiano the city of his birth. Go shopping and visit the museums. It'd do you good."

"Tag along like an extra piece of luggage?" she scoffed. "No, thanks! I've had enough of being made to feel small and insignificant. I'd rather stay here."

He knew her run-in with his mother lay behind her response, and if he was half the man he liked to think he was, he'd have shown more understanding. But he had bigger issues to resolve. The company his great-grandfather had created was hemorrhaging money and it had to be stopped. So instead of giving her the reassurance he knew she needed, to his horror and later regret, he heard himself roar, "Well, at least you can always call on the obliging Monsieur Gauthier to keep you company if the nights prove too long and lonely."

She blanched. *"What?"* she gasped.

"You heard me."

"Yes," she said after a pause, her eyes welling with tears. "I imagine half the island probably did."

Doing his best to moderate his tone, he said, "You're not the only one who's tired of our being apart more than we're together, Maeve. If I wanted to live like a bachelor, I wouldn't have married you in the first place."

"Perhaps that was your big mistake," she said, struggling to keep her voice steady. "But since you did, and since you have so little trust in me, perhaps the best thing you can do is put an end to what was never a love match in the first place."

And leave the door open for some half-assed wannabe artist to move onto his turf? Like hell! "Regardless of the reason for our marriage, the fact remains that it happened, and I have done my best to make it work. You have unlimited freedom and the wherewithal to enjoy it pretty much however you please. So forget any ideas you have of walking out on it. That is not, nor will it ever be an option."

"Watch me!" she spat. "I don't care how rich and famous you are, I will not sink back into that pathetic, browbeaten creature I once was, just for the privilege of being the great Dario Gabriele Costanzo's charity bride."

"I didn't marry you because I felt sorry for you, Maeve."

She swiped at the tears running down her face. "Oh, we all know very well why you married me," she said bitterly. "You had to do the right thing."

"Yes. Doing the right thing has always been important to me."

"Then how do you explain this?" Seizing a tabloid magazine lying on the coffee table, she thrust it at him. It fell open at a photograph showing him leaving a restaurant apparently in the company of blond, tanned beauty wearing a white dress so minuscule, it was barely decent.

"I can't," he said, tossing the magazine aside. "I won't lie to you. When I'm away, I'm frequently entertained by business men and their wives, many of whom are extremely attractive, but this woman is not one of them. I have no idea who she is nor, to my certain knowledge, have I ever so much as spoken a word to her."

"You didn't spend much time speaking to me, either, the night we met," she sobbed, "but that didn't stop you from—"

"I'm well aware how that night ended, Maeve. I made a mistake and I'm doing my best to live with it. But if you're determined to point fingers, let me remind you that at least some of the blame lay with you. All you ever had to say was stop."

Livid with himself and with her, he left her then, stopped just long enough to grab his briefcase from his desk, and strode out to the car. Within the hour he was onboard the company jet, headed for Milan.

The next afternoon the police contacted him. There'd been an accident. A car had spun out of control and gone over the edge of a cliff, some five or six kilometers from the villa on Pantelleria. Sebastiano had suffered minor injuries, Maeve was clinging to life, and the driver, Yves Gauthier, was dead.

CHAPTER TEN

GLOOMILY, Maeve watched as the aircraft gained height and headed due east over the Mediterranean. Too soon the Tunisian coastline sank into the hazy sunset distance and the black dot that was Pantelleria assumed more distinctive shape and color.

The day had flown by. She'd woken first and spent a minute or two inspecting the man she'd married. His face was more vulnerable in sleep, making him appear less the powerful business magnate. She loved the lean, firm line of his jaw, even dusted as it was with new-beard growth, and the way his black hair, normally so well behaved, spilled riotously over his forehead. She loved his strong neck, his dark, dense lashes that were enough to make a woman weep with envy, the sweeping arc of his eyebrows. She loved his mouth, its shape, its texture and its amazing talent as an instrument of seduction.

More than all that, she loved the inherent strength of him, the kind that had to do with something other than muscle and sinew. She might not remember their past relationship, but she knew instinctively that she could count on him. He was not a man to shirk his duty, renege on a promise or betray a friend. Although undoubtedly handsome as a god and sexier than was good for him or her, his real beauty came from within, and that was what she loved most about him.

Love…a word so often spoken without thought for what it should mean, yet sometimes the *only* word that would do, even if she couldn't recall it ever having crossed Dario's lips since their reunion. Yet perhaps that wasn't so strange, given that although they'd been married for over a year, because of her illness she'd really only known him for the last few weeks. Was it possible to fall in love with him all over again in so short a time, or was the up-swell of emotion he aroused in her something her heart remembered, even if her brain did not?

He stirred, stretched and raised his eyelids to half-mast, as if the weight of their lashes was more than they could be expected to cope with so early in the day. *"Buon giorno,"* he muttered, his voice so raspy and sensual that she tingled all over. "You have the look of a woman with much on her mind."

"I was just thinking."

"About?"

"What I'd like for breakfast."

"Come up with any ideas?"

"Yes," she said, drawing the sheet down past his waist and very precisely placing the tip of her forefinger exactly where she wanted it to go on his very male anatomy. "I'd like you."

His gray eyes darkened. "Help yourself, *amore mio*. I'm all yours."

After such a start to the morning, the famed mosaics in the Bardo Museum, which they visited later, weren't nearly as impressive as they might otherwise have been.

"I don't want to go back there," she said now, the words

falling into a silence broken only by the hum of the airplane's engines.

Dario looked up from the newspaper he was reading. "That's not what you told me yesterday. Yesterday you were captivated by Tunis."

"You don't understand," she said. "What I mean is, I don't want to go back to Pantelleria. Please, Dario, can't we go straight to Milan instead? I want to see my other home, and I can't believe you'd rather be trying to run your end of the business from the villa when it would be so much more efficient and convenient to be at the heart of things at corporate headquarters."

"Are you sure you're ready for such a radical step?" he asked her doubtfully. "Milan's a big city, and there was a time that you preferred the slower pace of life on Pantelleria."

"Not anymore," she said, with an inward shudder. "Antonia and the rest of the household staff have been most kind, and I don't mean to sound ungrateful, but I want to be around people who don't look at me as if I'm some sort of walking freak, or treat me as if I might break if I don't follow the exact same routine every day. Plus, we're almost into the second week of October now, and you said yourself there's not much to do on the island once summer's over."

"True. And with the fall fashion season getting underway in Milan, you'd enjoy seeing what's on the runway, I'm sure."

The chance to witness creative design at its most innovative transfused her with a well-remembered excitement. "Oh, I would!"

He rolled up the paper and regarded her thoughtfully.

"What?" she said, wishing she could read his mind.

"I'm wondering if there's something else you might be interested in, as well. Next Saturday is our company's annual benefit to raise awareness of *Parchi Per Bambini,* my great-grandfather's children's charity, which is as important today as it was when he first introduced it. There are now more than a hundred playgrounds in the poorer areas of various cities around the country, but not as many as we'd like to see, especially in the south. It'll be quite the gala occasion. How do you feel about attending it with me?"

"I'd love to."

"Think twice it before you say that. The whole family will be there, which you might find overwhelming since it'll be like meeting them all for the first time."

She grimaced. "Except for your mother. She and I, if you recall, already renewed our acquaintance with a singular lack of success, I might add."

"*Sì.* Except for my mother."

"Well, I have to face her again sooner or later, and the same goes for the others."

"You didn't feel that way a couple of weeks ago."

"A couple of weeks ago I hadn't rediscovered my marriage." Or fallen in love with her husband all over again. But perhaps it was too soon to tell him that, so she said instead, "I'm not the same woman I was back then."

"No, I don't believe you are. You're emerging from a chrysalis into a butterfly more than ready to spread her wings." He slapped the newspaper against his knee. "*D'accordo!* It's a date. I'll send for the company jet and we'll fly to Milan in the morning."

At last, no more marking time! Elation and relief fizzed

through her blood like champagne. She was a step away from rediscovering the other half of her lost life; hopefully one free of covert glances from anxious domestics, and secrets hidden behind locked doors.

"Well, this is it." Stepping out of the elevator, which they'd entered from a sunny private courtyard, Dario flung open the double doors to the penthouse.

Maeve stepped into a small marble foyer and paused, more than a little dazzled by what lay beyond. If the island villa was luxurious, this residence was palatial. Gleaming hardwood floors and paneled white walls graced an entrance hall grand enough to host a sixteenth-century masked ball. At one end, a spiral staircase rose to a gallery, above which a beveled glass dome flooded the entire area with natural light.

Apparently unnerved by her silence, Dario touched her arm tentatively. "If you're concerned at being left alone, I'll cancel my meeting," he offered, referring to the in-flight phone call he'd received after they'd left Pantelleria.

"Don't be silly," she said. "What do I have to be nervous about? The place isn't haunted, is it?"

"Not that I'm aware of."

"Then go with an easy mind."

"The meeting shouldn't last more than an hour or two, but call if you need anything. My assistant will put you through right away. Meanwhile, pour yourself a glass of wine and make yourself at home while I'm gone. I called ahead and had the maid service stock up the refrigerator. Better yet, take a nap. We left Pantelleria pretty early and you're probably tired."

Tired? She'd never felt more energized in her life, at least that she could recall. "Really, Dario, stop worrying. I'll be perfectly fine."

"All right, then." He hugged her and dropped a kiss on her mouth. "We'll go somewhere nice for lunch when I get back," he promised, the look in his eyes suggesting lunch wasn't the only thing he had in mind.

"I look forward to it." She shooed him away, eager to reacquaint herself with her sort-of-new home. "Now go!"

She waited until the elevator doors whispered closed behind him before passing through the entrance hall and an arched opening flanked by marble pillars to the living room—except so mundane a term scarcely did justice to the gracious expanse confronting her.

Elaborate white moldings stood in stark contrast to walls covered with burgundy-colored silk damask. Oil paintings, some portraits, some landscapes, hung in heavy carved frames. Thick ivory carpets cushioned the floors. An ebony grand piano stood in one corner, its highly polished lid reflecting the graceful fronds of a tall areca palm in a Chinese jardiniere. The remaining furniture was antique, Italian provincial mostly, with the sofas and armchairs upholstered in cream silk brocade. In the center of one wall was an elegant marble fireplace. The remaining walls boasted French doors that opened onto a wrap-around terrace with breathtaking views of the Duomo.

Pillared archways on either side of the fireplace gave access to a formal dining room large enough to seat a dinner party of twelve. A magnificent chandelier hung above the long table, its crystal prisms shooting fiery sparks in the bright sunlight. A butler's pantry connected this room to a superbly outfitted kitchen with a small but charming breakfast room set off to one side. There, another door opened directly into the big entrance hall.

Upstairs were three bedrooms each with its own marble bathroom. A four-poster occupied pride of place in the master suite, which also had a recessed sitting area set up with two arm-chairs. More ornate white molding showcased deep-ocher walls, with matching watered-silk drapes at the tall casement windows.

All comfort and luxury aside, though, the most interesting item, at least to Maeve, was a silver-framed photograph she found on a bureau. It showed her and Dario at some social function that required them both to wear evening dress. Although the camera had captured only their heads and shoul-ders, his black bow tie, starched white dress shirt with its pointy collar and the silk lapels of his dinner jacket were visible, as was the opal and silver or platinum filigree pendant nestled in the vee-shaped neck of her off-the-shoulder dark blue gown. Dario was suave sophistication personified, his smile dazzling and assured. Maeve wore the look of a deer caught in the headlights.

"I had a lot more cleavage in those days," she mused, taking a closer look at the picture, "and a lot more hair."

A quick survey of her dressing room told another story. Numerous famous designers were represented in all their expen-sive glory, filling the mirrored closets with outfits to suit every occasion. Stiletto-heeled shoes, jeweled evening sandals and limited-edition ankle boots lined the shoe racks, with handbags to match on a shelf above. All were designer labels she'd long admired and even coveted, but never expected to own. That she did so now was, she recognized, entirely thanks to Dario.

Overwhelmed by his unstinting generosity, she retraced her steps through the various rooms. His largesse went much farther than the contents of her wardrobe. The opulence surrounding her exceeded anything she could have imagined and quite how she'd managed to wipe all memory of it from her mind defied explanation. The girl who'd grown up in a tidy little rancher in east Vancouver had come a long way, and once upon a time such splendor would have intimidated her. Now the rich, warm colors and sumptuous textures seemed to fold themselves around her and welcome her in a manner that the cool blues and grays of the villa on Pantelleria never had. She felt at home. Safe and secure. Mistress of her own house, with no dark shadows peering over her shoulder.

Grateful beyond words for Dario having agreed to let her come here and for giving their marriage another boost, she racked her brains, trying to come up with a way to show her appreciation. She wanted to present him with something that didn't depend on wealth or position, both of which he had in abundance, but with a simple gift that came straight from her heart.

Finding herself back in the kitchen again, inspiration struck. As a teenager her other great interest, apart from designing and sewing her own clothes, had been cooking. Many a time she'd helped her mother make the big Sunday dinner, learning the importance of a light hand with pastry, the art of folding ingredients to create the perfect cake, and the secret of using herbs and spices to turn an otherwise bland sauce into a treat for the tastebuds. But as the wife of Dario Costanzo, multimillionaire and international business magnate, she'd never so much as made toast. At least, not in recent weeks. But as of today that was about to change.

Dario had mentioned having the maid service stock up on supplies, but a quick inspection of the refrigerator revealed only wine, cheese, grapes and coffee beans. Granted, there were oranges and bananas in a bowl on the granite counter, and a selection of crackers and biscotti in the cupboards, but that didn't exactly amount to what she'd call a well-stocked pantry, so she grabbed her purse and went shopping.

She found what she was looking for tucked into a narrow street behind the Plaza Duomo. A delicatessen with a few iron tables and chairs under an awning outside lured her over the threshold with the astonishing selection of gourmet foods she glimpsed through its open door. Braids of garlic hung from the ceiling. Olive oils, aromatic vinegars, foie gras, truffles and preserves lined one shelf; chocolates, another. Baskets of fresh bread stood on the counter. Trays of cooked poultry, smoked meats, cheeses and other dairy products were arranged in refrigerated display cases.

She made her choices and within the hour was home again, which, by her reckoning, left her exactly one hour more in which to whip together a meal and set the scene. She managed it all with minutes to spare before Dario showed up at half past one.

"What's all this?" he asked, stepping out to the terrace and surveying the table she'd set with dark green linens, white china and a small arrangement of white roses she'd bought from a street flower seller.

She handed him a glass of chilled white wine. "I made us lunch," she said, so proud of herself she was fit to burst. "I thought, seeing that it's such a lovely day, it would be nice to eat here."

"But I said I'd take you out."

"I decided to save you the trouble."

Mystified, he shook his head. "Costanzo wives don't cook for their husbands."

"This one does." She ushered him to the table. "Sit and enjoy your wine while I serve."

"We hire maids to do that."

"Not today," she said, and hurried back to the kitchen to put the finishing touches to the main dish.

Following her, he leaned against the center island and watched, bemused as she drizzled toasted almond slivers over chicken breasts coated with tarragon-flavored cream sauce. "I didn't know you could cook."

"Unlike you, I didn't grow up surrounded by servants, Dario. I can cook and clean house if I have to."

"Not our house, you can't. I draw the line at that."

"Really?" She angled a smile his way. "Were you always this bossy, or is it because I'm showing some independence that you're suddenly oozing testosterone from every pore?"

"Is that what I'm doing?"

"Well, let's just say you're being very much the macho Italian. It wouldn't surprise if, any minute how, you started beating your chest."

He lowered his lashes and favored her with an outrageously lascivious leer. "I'd rather beat yours."

"Behave yourself," she said severely. "And if you insist on getting in my way, make yourself useful and slice the bread."

"You'll be making me wear an apron next," he grumbled,

brandishing the bread knife with an expertise that told her he wasn't quite as averse to the domestic arts as he'd like her to believe.

"An excellent idea." Not missing a beat, she took off her apron, a pretty flowered affair with a ruffle along the hem, which she'd picked up in an open-air market near the delicatessen, and tied it around his waist.

Abandoning the bread, he pinned her between him and the center island. "Now you've gone too far, *principessa*. It's time I taught you a lesson."

She tried to wriggle free, at which his pupils flared and a splash of color stained the skin along his cheekbones. "Know what it's like to make love on a kitchen counter, Maeve?" he inquired, his voice raw and dangerous with desire.

Breathless herself, she whispered. "I don't imagine it'd be very comfortable."

He kissed her so hard she went weak at the knees. "Then stop tempting fate and serve me my lunch. Your punishment can wait until later."

The uninhibited banter and passion of that day left its mark on those that followed. With no household staff to monitor their comings and goings, they lived like ordinary people.

She wore her bathrobe to make him breakfast, and if he sometimes pulled her onto his lap when she went to serve him his espresso, and the coffee grew cold as a result, she didn't complain. He came home for lunch and often didn't return to his office until late in the afternoon, again because, somehow or other, he became distracted.

Occasionally they went out for dinner, once to a restaurant

at the top of a building so tall that it brought them face-to-face with the gargoyles on the Duomo. Another time he took her to an elegant place in the Piazza Republica where they enjoyed an exquisite five-course meal.

On the Thursday she went shopping for something to wear to the benefit. Despite the selection in her dressing room, the evening dresses were more suited for winter or spring wear, and the October weather was still mild. "Use it to buy whatever you want," Dario instructed, pressing a credit card into her hand before he left for the office that morning.

"You're spoiling me."

"It pleases me to do so, *amore mio,*" he returned.

She found the perfect gown in an atelier showroom on the Via Montenapoleone. Made from yard upon yard of ivory chiffon lined in silk, it fell from a strapless bodice nipped in at the waist to a cloud of airy swirls at her feet. Given her fair skin, she'd normally have chosen a deeper shade of fabric, but the delicate color complemented the golden tan she'd acquired on Pantelleria.

She didn't need accessories. She had the bejewelled sandals in her closet and enough evening purses to stock her own boutique. But her hair needed attention, and upon Dario's insistence, she made a Saturday-morning appointment at a very exclusive salon spa. Massage, facial, manicure, pedicure and hairdo, she had them all, with champagne served on the side, along with a tray of little appetizers to keep up her strength.

Such pampering! she thought, amused. In the old days she'd have fixed her own hair and painted her own nails, and done a creditable enough job of both. But tonight was too important for amateur efforts. She wanted so badly to be beautiful for Dario, and was desperate to win favor with his family.

When she emerged from her dressing room a few minutes before they were to leave for the benefit, she knew all the effort had been worthwhile. For once he was speechless and simply stared at her as if he'd never seen her before.

"Look at you," he finally said, his gaze roaming from the top of her head where the stylist had coaxed her hair into a smooth, upswept golden coil, to the jeweled sandals on her feet. "*Una signora cosi bella* and all mine."

"Does that mean you won't be embarrassed to introduce me to your family again?"

"Embarrassed?" He took her chin between his thumb and forefinger and dropped a reverent kiss on her mouth. "Maeve, *innamorata,* I could not be more proud."

His approval buoyed her up during the drive to the hotel where the benefit was being held. It sustained her when he offered his elbow and escorted her into the room adjacent to the ballroom, where a well-dressed crowd was enjoying pre-dinner cocktails. It gave her the courage to meet the discreet stares of strangers, and fortified her enough that she was able to smile when he led her to a group gathered off to one side.

At their approach, an older man with thick silver hair and dark gray eyes like Dario's stepped forward.

"My father, Edmondo," Dario murmured.

"Buona sera, signor," she said, horribly aware of being the center of attention of just about everyone in the room, most particularly Dario's mother, whose expression suggested she'd been assaulted by an unpleasant odor.

"What is this *signor* all about?" his father exclaimed, embracing Maeve warmly. "You might have forgotten that you once called me *Papa,* but I have not."

His kindness, especially in the face of his wife's overt hostility, made Maeve's eyes sting with incipient tears. "Oh," she said, and cringed at her inane response.

"And my sister, Giuliana," Dario continued, bracing her with an arm at her waist.

"Maeve, *cara!*" His sister swept her into a hug that pretty much squeezed the breath from her lungs, but went a long way toward restoring her equilibrium. "I am so happy to see you again. You look wonderful, doesn't she, Lorenzo?"

"*Sì,*" the tall man who was with her agreed, and brushed a kiss over both Maeve's cheeks. "*Ciao,* Maeve. We have all missed you."

Throughout the introductions, Dario's mother continued to observe her disdainfully. "This is an unexpected turn of events, Dario," she finally announced, in a stage whisper that probably carried as far as Pantelleria. "Are you sure it was wise to bring her here?"

"And you've met my mother, of course," he said smoothly, the chilly glare he bestowed on Celeste enough to turn her to stone.

"Yes." Rallying her pride, Maeve extended her hand. "How very nice to see you again, Signora Costanzo."

No affectionate hug from that quarter, or offer to call her *Madre.* Not that Maeve wanted to. Celeste Costanzo was about as far removed from the mother she'd loved so dearly as chalk was from cheese.

"Indeed," Celeste replied. "And may I say how very nice

it is to see you more appropriately attired than when we last crossed paths."

The rest of Dario's family might have been happy to see her again, but any hope Maeve had nursed that she and her mother-in-law might make a fresh start died at that. Before the evening so much as got underway, the battle lines had been drawn.

CHAPTER ELEVEN

KEEPING an eye on Maeve, who went into dinner on his father's arm, Dario pulled Giuliana aside and, under cover of the general buzz of conversation surrounding them, asked, "How's Sebastiano? It's been over a week since I last saw him, but it feels more like months."

"He's fine, Dario. As I told you when we spoke this morning, we left him and Cristina with Marietta because we saw no point in dragging them all the way from the island just for one night. But earlier this evening, Lorenzo phoned her to find out how they were doing, and both children were already in bed and asleep. They'll hardly have time to miss us before we're home again."

"While his mother continues to live in ignorance of his very existence." Dario ground his teeth in frustration. "I don't know how much longer I can go on like this, Giuliana. I miss my son."

"But you have your wife back, and that's progress, surely?"

"I tell myself it is and certainly she's seemed much happier this last week. If it weren't for the fact that we have a child, I could let the past go and build on what we've got now. As it is, we're in a holding pattern, waiting for something to jog her memory, and who's to say what that might mean? She could decide she wants no part of me or our marriage."

"I seriously doubt that'll ever happen. She wears the look of a woman in love with her husband."

"Even assuming you're right, love based on misconceptions doesn't stand much chance of surviving, once the truth comes out. I'm deliberately keeping her from her baby. If the situation were reversed, I would find that impossible to forgive."

"You're following her doctor's advice, Dario."

"Barely. Sometimes I come so close to ignoring everything Peruzzi believes is the right way to go about things that it's all I can do not to simply tell her exactly how the accident came about, and let the chips fall where they may."

"Then why don't you?"

"Because it could destroy her. You and I both know self-esteem isn't her strong suit. Unfortunately, patience isn't one of mine."

His sister touched his arm sympathetically. "You must be doing something right, Dario. She's positively glowing."

"For now," he said. "But who knows how long that will last, once her memory returns?"

Weaving his way deftly through the crowd, Edmondo led Maeve to a table at the far end of the ballroom and handed her into her chair with courtly, old-world charm. "Here we are, *cara mia*. I'm putting you next to me in order for us to get to know each other again."

"And I," Lorenzo announced, taking the seat on her other side, "intend to do the same."

"I'm flattered," she said, and scanned the room, trying not

to betray how jittery she felt. She was out of her element in this smart, sophisticated crowd. "Where's Dario?"

"Mingling with his guests for a change," Celeste informed her loftily. "In his position, he can scarcely remain so frequently absent from the social scene and not expect to perform double duty when he does choose to appear."

"I'm afraid it's my fault he's spent so much time away, Signora Costanzo."

"We are well aware of the reason, my dear," Edmondo said, patting her hand kindly. "His first duty was, and is, to you, his wife, something we all understand."

All except for Celeste, Maeve thought, silently berating Dario for suggesting she attend this blasted affair, then leaving her to his mother's untender mercies.

Some of her dismay must have been apparent to Lorenzo because he leaned close and murmured, "Don't take Celeste's words to heart, Maeve. Her bark, as they say in English, is much worse than her bite."

"I'm not inclined to put the theory to the test."

Giuliana arrived at the table in time to overhear their exchange and laughed. "Smart lady," she said. "It takes most people years to arrive at that conclusion."

Following close behind, Dario stopped long enough to trace a discreetly intimate finger over the exposed skin of Maeve's back. "Sorry I left you to fend for yourself, *amore*. How are you doing?"

"Better now that you're here," she told him, her annoyance evaporating in the warmth of his touch.

"I'm yours for the rest of the night," he promised, giving

her shoulder a squeeze before taking his place between his mother and sister as a hovering waiter began to pour the wine.

When all the glasses were filled, Edmondo stood up, cleared his throat and turned a benign glance Maeve's way. "This date has long held special meaning for me because it was my grandfather's birthday. I have always been proud of him for his efforts to improve the lot of those less fortunate than himself, and prouder still that my children continue to support the work he began. But I don't know that I've ever been prouder than I am tonight, when I look around this table and see my grown-up family complete again." He raised his glass. "I therefore ask you to join me in a toast to a very special young woman. To you, Maeve, and a full recovery very soon, *cara mia*. We have missed you."

Her father-in-law meant well, she knew, but the last thing Maeve wanted was to be the focus of everyone's attention. She hadn't liked it when she'd been singled out in high school, and she didn't like it now. In an agony of embarrassment she looked across the table to Dario, silently begging him to deflect the spotlight elsewhere.

He met her gaze and held it steady, his calm gray eyes telling her she was not alone, and that whatever surprises the evening might bring, he'd be beside her and together they'd cope. He made it possible for her to breathe air into her beleaguered lungs and unclench her fingers, which lay knotted in her lap. Because of him she was able to return Edmondo's smile, murmur her thanks and not mind too terribly much that Celeste barely managed to acknowledge the toast without gagging.

At length Edmondo sat down again, and general conversation resumed as a melon-and-prosciutto appetizer, the first of several courses, was presented. A delicate chicken consommé came next, followed by artichoke salad with capers brought all the way from Pantelleria, then scampi on a bed of braised endive. Before the entree, palate-cleansing basil and lime sorbet appeared in thimble-size stemmed glasses.

Somehow, Maeve was able to manage it all without dribbling, drooling, using the wrong fork or otherwise embarrassing herself—this, despite having Celeste watch her the entire time like a hawk waiting to pounce on a rabbit. Of course, it helped that throughout the feast, Dario also captured Maeve's glance and smiled a private little smile, one so loaded with sensual promise that she was almost able to ignore Celeste's hooded scrutiny.

Between courses, with a lift of one eyebrow and a meaningful nod at other couples gliding around the floor to the strains of the orchestra, he invited her to dance. She melted dreamily in his arms, her pretty dress floating around her ankles like morning mist, and lost herself in the spicy scent of his aftershave and the firm reassurance of his body pressed close to hers. She wished the evening would never end, at the same time that she wanted it to be over so that they'd be alone again.

He scattered tiny kisses against her brow. Held her ever closer and told her how proud she made him, how beautiful she was. And when the chandeliers dimmed and the music slowed to a sultry beat, he drew her closer still and whispered other things in her ear. Shocking, sexy, outrageously thrilling things not meant for anyone else to hear.

With his every wicked word, desire built, streaming through her blood and leaving her body and spirits soaring. Suspended in breathless anticipation.

Perhaps she soared too high. How else to account for her clumsiness when she returned to the table after a particularly stirring slow waltz, and somehow managed to knock over Lorenzo's wine? One second she was easing into her chair, preparing to enjoy the medallion of filet mignon on her plate; the next, the glass was tilting in precarious slow motion and the contents spilling out to leave the front of her gown stained a dark purplish-red.

"Oh, my goodness!" she cried, mopping ineffectually at the river of wine still trickling into her lap. "Lorenzo, I'm so sorry."

"Not at all," he insisted with impeccable courtesy. "My fault entirely."

But it wasn't. She knew it, and so did everyone else at the table, except for Giuliana, whose seat was empty. A well-bred commotion arose: Dario summoning a waiter to rectify a situation beyond repair; Edmondo gently insisting such things happened and no one was to blame; Lorenzo apologizing needlessly, again and again. And a sudden hush from nearby tables as attention shifted to the drama unfolding at the Costanzos'.

Maeve shriveled inside and wished she could die. Aware of all eyes on her, the anonymity she craved again denied her, she muttered her excuses, stumbled awkwardly to her feet and fled, her brief Cinderella reign at an end.

The ladies' room, smothered in the scented silence of gardenias, was as elegantly appointed as the ballroom. Low white leather benches on spindly legs fronted a long marble vanity topped by a beveled mirror. Crystal wall scones shed a flattering light.

Too much light! One glance at her reflection revealed with

glaring accuracy in its unwinking surface, the extent of Maeve's fall from grace. Her dress was ruined. The wine had seeped right through the chiffon to the silk lining, putting paid to any far-fetched notion she'd entertained that sponging it with cold water might be able to effect a miracle. She could have wept.

Behind her, the door whispered open and to her added horror, Celeste appeared. *Ah, no,* Maeve thought in despair. *Not this, not now!*

Her mother-in-law glided across the thick carpet, subjected Maeve to a pitying stare and, without so much as a word, took a wand of lip gloss from her beaded purse and applied fresh color to her mouth.

Her silence condemned more thoroughly than any verbal attack she might have launched. Unable to bear it, Maeve said haltingly, "It *was* an accident, Signora Costanzo."

Celeste snapped her lipstick closed and leaned forward to inspect herself in the mirror. "You're rather fond of accidents, it would seem," she drawled.

Maeve sucked in a shocked breath. "Are you saying you think I did this on purpose?"

"I think you're a magnet for disaster, which follows you wherever you go. The pity of it is, it touches the people around you, as my son has discovered to his cost."

Chagrined, Maeve said, "Have I never managed to do anything right in your eyes?"

"You used to dress well enough at least to *look* the part of a Costanzo wife." Celeste's gaze skimmed over her, coldly, pitilessly. "Now you can't even do that."

Although Maeve stood at least three inches taller than her

mother-in-law, at that moment she felt herself shrink into an old, all too familiar insignificance. "I have tried to fit in," she said.

Celeste let out a snort of contempt. "You will never fit in. You're a nobody."

"You're quite right," Maeve said, stung into retaliating. "I was not born with a silver spoon in my mouth. I come from very humble origins. But my parents had their priorities straight. They understood what common decency was all about, and instilled in me a sense of humanity you completely lack. What kind of woman rejects another for something beyond her control? More to the point, what kind of *mother are you,* that you refuse to accept your son's wife?"

Celeste turned white around the mouth. "You have the effrontery to lecture me about how a mother should behave? You, who has turned over responsibility for her—"

"That's enough, *Madre!*" Suddenly Giuliana was there, inserting herself between them. "Not another word, do you hear? Maeve, *mia sorella la più cara,* Dario sent me to find you. Come with me now."

"No," Maeve said, standing her ground. "Not until she finishes what she started to say."

"It is not my mother's place to say anything," Giuliana insisted, grasping her by the elbow and marching her to the door. "This is between you and Dario. Let him be the one to answer your questions."

Shaking from the aftermath of her confrontation with Celeste, Maeve whispered, "How can I face him? This evening is such an important occasion for your family, and I spoiled it."

"You did no such thing." Opening the door, Giuliana

almost shoved her out to where Dario waited. "Get her away from here," she told him urgently. "In fact, get her out of town quickly, before our mother finds a way to finish what she just started. Enough damage has been done for one night."

He nodded, wrapped Maeve's velvet evening cape around her shoulders and ushered her from the hotel to his chauffeured car parked in the forecourt. Bundling her into the backseat, he climbed in after her, slammed closed the door and told his driver, *"A Linate."*

Linate was the airport where the corporate jet had landed on its arrival from Pantelleria, her island prison. "Are we going back to the villa?" she asked in numb resignation.

"No," he said. "We're going back to Portofino, where we began."

"Why bother? It won't change who I am."

"You're my wife."

"Take a good look at me, Dario," she said, throwing open her cape, while the tears she'd so far managed to suppress flooded her eyes. The city streetlights flashed intermittently over her ruined evening gown, turning the stain dark as blood. "I'm a pathetic misfit."

He folded her hands between his and chafed them. "It's only a dress, Maeve," he said gently. "Not worth getting upset about."

"Oh, it's about so much more than that, and we both know it. It's my life, disguised under a veneer of high-society money and sophistication to hide who I really am underneath. Your mother's right. I don't belong with a man like you. You should let me go and find someone from your own strata of society to be your wife."

"It's much too late for that."

"Why?"

He hesitated, and she realized how often he'd done that in response to her questions over the last weeks, as though he had to launder his answer before daring to utter it.

Beside herself, she struck out at his arm with her fist. "Tell me!" she cried. "If it concerns me, I have the right to know."

"Okay!" He threw up his hands in surrender. "But not until we get to Portofino. You've waited this long to hear the whole story. Another hour or two isn't going to make any difference to the outcome."

He'd called ahead for a helicopter to transport them to Rappallo, and for one of his sailing crew to open up the yacht and have a car waiting to drive them the short distance from the heliport to Portofino.

Maeve was shivering by the time they'd taken the dinghy out to the big boat and climbed aboard, though whether from the cool night air or sheer misery was hard to determine. Not that it made any difference to Dario. He'd held out long enough and it was time to come clean. Peruzzi could say what he liked about waiting for nature to take its course, but Peruzzi wasn't the one watching Maeve come unraveled.

Taking her to the aft salon on the promenade deck, he filled two mugs with the hot chocolate he'd ordered prepared, then carried them to where she huddled on the couch and sat down next to her. "Here," he said. "This will warm you up."

She brought her hands out from under her cape and wrapped them around the mug. "Thanks," she said dully. It was the first word she'd uttered since her impassioned plea for the truth, during the drive to Linate.

Her gaze flickered around the salon, and after a while she spoke again. "Is this room where we began?"

"Not quite. We spent that night on deck."

"Tell me about it."

So he did, leaving out nothing. No point trying to whitewash the facts at this stage. He'd behaved badly and she might as well know that from the start.

She sipped her hot chocolate and listened without interrupting until he finished, then said, "So we had sex the first night we met?"

"I prefer to say we made love."

Her face registered her disbelief. "How could I have done that? I'd never been with a man before."

"I know," he said.

"Being saddled with a novice couldn't have been much fun for you."

"*Fun* isn't the word that comes to mind, Maeve." Taking her mug, he set it with his on the low table in front of them and clasped her hands. "Even in your innocence, you were passionate and generous, and I couldn't resist you. But I admit I was taken aback when I realized I was your first lover. You were twenty-eight at the time and beautiful. How is it you were still a virgin?"

"I didn't have much time for romance. I was too busy building a career." She looked at him almost shyly. "I'm glad there's only ever been you."

Had there? Or would she remember another lover, before the night ended?

"So what happened next?" she went on. "Did we know right from the start that we were meant to be together?"

Hearing the sudden lilt in her voice, he averted his gaze. "It didn't happen quite like that. You left for home a few days later and I didn't expect to see you again. But I found you weren't easy to forget."

"Forgetting's always easy. It's the remembering that's hard."

Thinking back to the day he'd proposed, he had to admit that in a way she was right. He'd give his right arm not to remember what happened next....

Late on a stinking hot afternoon at the end of August, he stopped in Vancouver on his way from Seattle to Whistler. Tracking her down was simple enough. There was only one Maeve Montgomery, Personal Shopper, listed in the Vancouver business pages.

She lived in the city's west end, on the sixth floor of a west-facing apartment building in English Bay. The beach was littered with sunbathers soaking up the rays when he arrived. Mothers unpacked picnic hampers and spread towels over huge logs washed up by winter tides. Children held their fathers' hands and splashed in the shallow waves rolling ashore, their shrieks of glee occasionally rising above the muted roar of commuter traffic headed for the suburbs.

A pleasant enough spectacle of domesticity, but not something that held much appeal for him, he decided, searching for Maeve's name in the list of residents posted next to the intercom outside her front door. There were too many beautiful women in the world for him to tie himself down to just one; women who understood how the game of love was played.

Is that why you're here, because Maeve Montgomery's one

of those women? The question came at him out of nowhere just as he was about to buzz her number.

He stopped with his finger poised. What the devil was he thinking? They had nothing in common, beyond a night they both wanted to forget. Why would she want to see him again? More to the point, why did he want to see her? For a romp between the sheets, when he knew that's all it would ever amount to for him? To boost his ego at the expense of hers, *again?*

Disgusted with himself, he turned away. At the bottom of the steps, a leggy blond in shorts and a sleeveless T-shirt had stopped to balance a brown paper sack of groceries on one hip while she fumbled in a leather bag hanging from her other shoulder. The setting sun silhouetted the elegant jut of her hip, the curve of her bosom, the rounded swell of her belly.

Preoccupied with finding whatever she was looking for in the purse, she didn't notice him. But he had ample time to study her and what he saw filled him with black despair. The woman was Maeve, and she was unmistakably pregnant. About four and a half months along, he reckoned, recalling how his sister had looked at that stage when she was expecting Cristina. And the last time he'd seen Maeve had been in April….

He'd reached a critical point in his revelations. Either he plunged ahead with a truth that the experts had warned could crush her, or he stopped now and continued to pray for a miracle that he knew in his heart was not going to happen. Neither the island, Milan nor seeing his family again had triggered her memory. Portofino had been his last hope that he'd be spared having to tell her bluntly how they'd come to be husband and wife. And it, too, had drawn a blank.

Cool night air notwithstanding, he was sweating. Ripping off his bow tie, he undid the top two buttons of his shirt, strode out to the promenade deck and leaned on the rail, his chest heaving. The moon slid out from the shadow of the *castello* atop the steep hillside rising behind the town, and shed a pearly glow over the bell tower of the Church of San Giorgio. Closer at hand the sea lapped gently against the yacht's hull. But overriding them all was the scene unfolding in his memory....

Unaware that she was being watched, Maeve had hitched her purse strap more securely over her shoulder, shifted the sack of groceries to the crook of her arm and climbed the steps, a set of keys dangling from her free hand.

He waited until she reached the top before blocking her passage and, removing his sunglasses, said, "*Ciao*, Maeve."

She stopped dead, shock leaching the color from her face. Her mouth fell open, but no sound came forth. Her eyes grew huge and wary. At last, making a visible effort to collect herself, she asked faintly, "Why are you here?"

"I'd have thought that was self-evident. I've come to see you."

As if "come to see you" conveyed a message vastly different from the usual, she tried unsuccessfully to hide her thickened waist behind the sack of groceries. "I'm afraid this isn't a good time. I have other plans for tonight."

"Cancel them," he said flatly. "We obviously have matters to discuss."

"I thought I made it clear the last time we were together that I have nothing to say to you, Dario."

"That was nearly five months ago. Much has changed since then. For a start, you're pregnant."

"What's that got to do with anything?"

"Plenty, if, as I have reason to suspect, it's my baby you're carrying."

She tilted her chin proudly. "Just because you happened to be the first man I slept with doesn't mean you were the last."

"Quite possibly not," he agreed, "but nor does it address the question of the child's paternity."

A crimson flush chased away her pallor. "Are you suggesting I'm the kind of woman who doesn't know who her baby's father is?"

"No," he said pleasantly. "You came up with that improbable scenario all by yourself. And we both know you're lying because that same kind of woman doesn't wait until she's twenty-eight to part with her virginity."

"I'm twenty-nine now. Old enough to live my life without your help, so please go back to wherever you came from."

"I don't care if you're a hundred," he snarled, infuriated by her attitude. "I'm going nowhere until we've established if I'm the one who got you pregnant, so hand over your groceries, lead the way to your apartment, and let's continue this conversation someplace a little less public."

"Don't order me around. I'm not your servant."

"No," he said wearily. "But we both know you're the mother of my child, and whether or not you like it, that gives me the right to a lot more than you appear willing to recognize, so quit stalling and open the damned door."

She complied with a singular lack of grace and rode the elevator to the sixth floor in mutinous silence. Once in her apartment, she flung open the doors to the balcony to let in what little breeze came off the water, then spun around to face him. "All right, now what?"

"Now we talk like reasonable adults, beginning with your admitting the baby's mine."

"I was under the impression you'd already made up your mind you knew the answer to that."

"Nevertheless, I want to hear *you* acknowledge it."

"Fine." She slumped wearily onto a padded ottoman and eased off her sandals. "Congratulations. You're about to become a daddy, though quite how you managed it is something I'm still trying to figure out."

"The same way most men do," he said, her sulky indignation all at once leaving him hard-pressed not to smile. Which would have been inappropriate in more ways than one. She was in no mood to be teased, and there was nothing remotely amusing about the predicament they were facing.

"I didn't think a woman was likely to get pregnant her first time. In any case, you used a condom."

"Not quite soon enough, I'm afraid, and for that I have only myself to blame. I knew better than to run such a risk. My only excuse, and a poor one at that, is that I found you irresistible."

"Oh, please! Once it was over, you couldn't wait to be rid of me. The fact that you didn't once bother to contact me afterward is proof enough of that. Which brings me back to my original question. Why are you here?"

"You weren't as forgettable as you seem to assume. I was passing through the city and decided to look you up. Now that I am here, however, the question uppermost in my mind is, when were you planning to tell me about the pregnancy?"

"I wasn't. All you were interested in was a one-night stand, not a lifetime of responsibility."

"I might be every kind of cad you care to name, Maeve, but I'm not completely without conscience. You could have contacted me at any time through the Milan office, and I would have come to you."

"What makes you think I wanted you? I already have everything necessary to give my baby a nice, normal life."

"Not quite," he said. "You don't have a husband."

"I won't be the first single mother in town. Thousands of women take on the job every day and do it very well."

"Some mothers have no other choice, but you can't seriously believe a child isn't better off with two parents to love and care for him."

"No," she admitted, after a moment's deliberation. "If you want to be part of this baby's life, I won't try to stop you."

"How very generous of you," he said drily. "But explain to me if you will how that's going to work, with your living here and my being in Italy? A child is not a parcel to be shipped back and forth between us."

"You have a better solution?"

"Of course. We form a merger."

"Merger? As in, another company to add to your corporate assets?"

"Marry, then, if you prefer."

"What I'd prefer," she said tightly, bright spots of color dotting her cheeks, "is for you to take your *merger* and leave—preferably by way of a flying leap off the balcony!"

"I'm making you an honorable offer, Maeve."

"And I'm declining. I'm no more interested in acquiring a

reluctant husband than I'm quite sure you are in being saddled with a wife."

He looked at her. At her long, elegant legs, her shining blond hair, the fine texture of her skin and the brilliant blue of her eyes. She was beautiful, desirable, but so were any number of other women, none of whom had spurred him to relinquish his bachelor state in favor of married life. What made her forever different was the bulge beneath her T-shirt for which he was responsible. And in his book, that left him with only one choice.

"It's no longer just about us and what we want," he said. "Like it or not, we are to be a family, and to us Italians, family is everything."

"Well, I'm not Italian. I'm a liberated North American woman who well understands that even under ideal circumstances, marriage is hard work. And you can hardly expect me to believe you think these are ideal circumstances."

"They are unexpected," he conceded, "but not impossible."

And so it had gone back and forth between them for the next hour or more until, eventually, he had worn her down and she had accepted his proposal.

He took her out for dinner to celebrate. She hadn't eaten much because a late meal gave her heartburn. He hadn't eaten much because the enormity of what he now faced sat in his stomach like a lead weight....

The rustle of her gown and faint drift of her perfume brought him back to the present. "Dario?" she said, coming to where he stood at the rail and placing her hand on his arm. "What's wrong?"

He blew out a tormented breath. How did he begin to tell her?

CHAPTER TWELVE

HE DIDN'T answer, but stood as if carved from stone and refused to look at her. Already at the end of her rope, Maeve shook his arm in a burst of near-uncontrollable fury. "Don't ignore me!" she raged. "I asked you a straightforward question. *What's wrong?*"

A shudder ran through him. He inhaled sharply, opened his mouth to answer, then snapped it closed again.

Never in her life had she physically assaulted anyone. The very idea sickened her. But at that moment Maeve's frustration was such that it was all she could do not to kick and bite and scratch and do whatever else it took to jolt him into responding. But no, she thought, her anger subsiding into despair. Not just responding. Telling the whole truth for a change.

"Listen to me," she said, struggling to keep her voice from cracking. "This has to stop now. The searching gazes, the pregnant pauses…I'm tired of them all."

To her astonishment, he let out a bark of ironic laughter.

"You think this is funny?" she gasped.

"No," he said, sobering. "Just an unfortunate choice of words on your part, that's all."

"How so?"

Pushing himself away from the rail, he squared his shoulders and faced her with the dull resignation of a man confronting a firing squad. "Wait here. I'll be right back with the answer."

She watched him go, her insides churning. She wanted to know everything. Wanted it so passionately that it was eating her alive. Yet at the same time, she was afraid, as if, in the deepest recesses of her mind and heart, she knew she wouldn't be able to live with what she learned.

He was back within minutes. Beckoning her into the salon, he switched on a table lamp and gave her a rather large white envelope. "Here," he said. "If it's true that a picture's worth a thousand words, this should tell you plenty."

Inside was a photograph, the second she'd come across in the last week, this latest of her and Dario on their wedding day. It was almost as he'd described it. Almost. She recognized the Vancouver courthouse in the background, her blue dress, the little posy of white lilies and roses. But he'd neglected to mention one not-so-tiny detail that leaped out at her and left her light-headed with shock.

Surely, she thought, groping blindly for the couch, it was a mistake? A trick of light, an optical illusion?

She blinked to clear her vision, and looked again. The picture trembled in her hand like a storm-tossed leaf, but the incriminating evidence remained intact. "Dario," she whimpered in a voice she barely recognized, "are my eyes deceiving me, or was I pregnant?"

"They're not deceiving you," he said.

Then that had to mean…

Her entire body froze, trapped in the path of a conclusion

so gravely dark and terrible that to acknowledge it would crush the life out of her. So she attempted to deflect it by seeking escape in the trivial. *No wonder she'd sported such an impressive cleavage in the photograph taken last December. No wonder some of the clothes she'd found in her dressing room at the penthouse appeared so roomy. No wonder…no wonder…*

"And that's why you married me?" she continued, desperate to avoid uttering the word screaming to be heard. "Because you felt you had to?"

"Yes."

For weeks she'd begged him to answer her questions directly, and for weeks he'd edited the facts to spare her feelings. But now that she needed him to cushion the blow, he blasted her with a truth so painful that she cringed.

Scrutinizing the photo again, she said, "I guess that explains why you look so stony-faced."

"You weren't exactly radiant yourself. We had not planned to have a baby."

Baby, baby, baby…

There it was, out in the open, the word she'd so strenuously tried to ignore. And once spoken, it hovered in the atmosphere, a devastating, debilitating accusation that shot her from limbo straight into hell.

"What happened to it?" she whispered, caught in a web of indescribable horror. "Is that why I feel so empty inside—because I miscarried?"

"You didn't miscarry."

This time his stark reply pierced the heavy bank of fog that had been her constant companion for so long and shredded it to ribbons. They began to shift and part, letting in terrifying fragments of memory.

The salon grew dark and fearful, inhabited by ghosts that threatened to devour her. Moaning, she threaded her fingers through her hair and dug them into her scalp. Touched the scar now so well concealed. But the images and sounds leaked through its healed incision.

She relived the sudden jarring impact of a car leaving the road and careening out of control toward the edge of a cliff. Heard again the hideous shriek of tearing metal, the splintering of glass.

She saw the man beside her slumped over the wheel, and herself scrabbling wildly to release her seat belt so that she could climb into the back of the car, because her baby was there, imprisoned in his infant safety seat. Except it wasn't safe at all because the car was rocking and spinning, and she had to free him, had to get him out of there and save him, because he was her darling, her precious son, and she would give her life for him.

She saw the thin line of blood oozing down his pale, still face. Felt herself drowning in his terrifying, soul-screaming silence. And then the world was turning upside down, and the sea was rushing up to meet her, and there was nothing but darkness.

Until now, when the light of her failure shone too brightly before her and so many fragmented pieces came together to make a horrifying whole.

The locked room on the island had been his nursery, filled with magical things to entertain him and keep him safe. Mobiles and music boxes; soft blankets and tiny sleeper sets. A quilt she'd made before he was born. Lullabies she'd sung. Books she'd read to him, even though he was too young to understand the meaning: *Counting Kisses* and *Goodnight Moon*.

Oh, sweet heaven! Oh, dear God, please, *please*…!

The floor came up to meet her as she crumpled over, hugging herself to keep the pain from splitting her in half.

"Maeve?"

She was dimly aware of Dario sinking down beside her, his arms trying to draw her upright on the sofa, his voice layered with concern. In a fit of unprecedented agony, she sagged against him. "How can you bear to be near me?" she sobbed. "How can you bear to touch me? Because of me, our beautiful little boy is dead."

"Not so," he crooned, stroking her hair.

"He is," she wept, driven to near madness by her grief. "I remember it all." Her breath caught at the endless horror movie rolling through her mind. "Dario, I saw him."

Grasping her by the shoulders, he shook her gently but firmly. "Whatever you think you saw, Sebastiano is not dead, *amore mio*. Do you hear me? *He is not dead.*"

"You're lying," she cried, flailing wildly to break free from his hold. "You've been lying to me all along."

"Yes, I have lied," he admitted. "By omission. To protect you until you were ready to face the truth. But I would never lie about this. I give you my word that our son is alive and well."

Her adorable baby, with his gummy smiles and big blue eyes, whose skin was softer and sweeter smelling than a rose petal, was *not* alive. He couldn't be.

"His car seat saved him, Maeve."

"No," she said brokenly. "I saw the blood. I saw it, Dario."

"It was nothing. A minor cut caused by something flying loose in the car from the impact."

His certainty, the ring of truth in his words, let a crack of light into the darkness inhabiting her soul. "A minor cut? That was all?"

"Not quite. He suffered a bruised spleen, as well, and was hospitalized for a few days, but he's fine now. More than fine. He's thriving."

"Then, where is he?" she cried, her arms aching to hold him. "Why haven't I seen him since I left the hospital?"

"I sent him to live with my family until you were better."

"Your family?" She recoiled as if he'd slapped her. "If he's with your mother—"

"He's not with my mother. Giuliana has been looking after him on Pantelleria. He's there now, with her daughter and their nanny."

She hadn't thought Dario could shock her more than he already had, but the sheer audacity of his last disclosure took her breath away. "All this time he was practically living next door and you didn't tell me?" And to think she'd felt guilty about sneaking around behind *his* back! "How dare you!"

"Maeve…" He went to pull her into his arms.

She shook him off. "You kept him from me."

"From me, too, and if you think it was easy, you're wrong." He threw up his hands in surrender. "Stop looking so wounded. I did what I thought was best."

"Best for whom?"

"For you, Maeve. I thought—"

"I don't care what you thought. I want my son." The

wretched tears started again, weakening her when she most needed all her strength. "Damn you, I want my baby!"

"Tomorrow," he promised. "We'll go back to the island first thing tomorrow."

"No. I want to go to him now."

"Be reasonable, Maeve. It's after midnight. There's no way we can get there tonight."

"Sure there is. You're Dario Almighty Costanzo. You can charter a jet as easily as other men hail taxis. You can make a child disappear so that no trace of him remains to remind his mother he ever existed. How do I know you haven't sent him away where I'll never find him?"

"Don't be ridiculous," Dario said sharply. "I've done nothing of the sort. On the recommendation of your doctors, I hid all reminders of him until such time as you, of your own accord, were well enough to cope with the events that brought about the accident."

"You had no right. You're not God."

"No," he said. "I'm merely your husband, as subject to making mistakes as any other mortal. In hindsight, perhaps I did the wrong thing but at the risk of repeating myself ad nauseam, at the time, I thought I was acting in your best interests."

"When is keeping a mother from her child ever in anyone's best interests, Dario?" she asked bitterly.

"When the mother has been traumatized to the point that she has no recollection of giving birth," he suggested, then, regarding her steadily, went on, "Or perhaps if there is reason to believe that said mother intends to desert her husband and abscond with their child."

She stared at him, dumbfounded. *"Abscond?"*

"Run away," he amended helpfully.

"I understand what the word means," she snapped. "What I don't understand and certainly don't like is that you'd think me capable of such a thing."

"I don't like it, either, but the facts appeared to speak for themselves."

"What facts?" she said scornfully.

He subjected her to another steely gaze. "You had most of Sebastiano's things with you in that car, Maeve—his clothes, his favorite toys, even his baby swing—as well as a suitcase of your own stuff. You were with Yves Gauthier, a man who'd shown up out of nowhere in June and who'd insinuated himself into your life so thoroughly that everyone on the island was buzzing about it."

"We were fellow ex-pats. It was natural we should become friends."

"Was it natural for him to lease a villa for three months, then suddenly be headed for the airport within a few weeks, with a return ticket to Canada, via Rome, tucked inside his passport?"

"Did I have a ticket to Rome tucked in my passport? Come to that, did I even have my or Sebastiano's passport with me?"

"No. But in view of the fact that, the day before, you and I had had a flaming row at the end of which you told me in no uncertain terms to leave you the hell alone, you can scarcely blame me for entertaining doubts about what you had in mind."

"I remember our arguing," she said, the sequence of events falling into place with disturbing accuracy. "We fought because you wanted me to come back to Milan with you, and I said I wouldn't because that meant putting up with your mother forever interfering and trying to take over with Sebastiano. You said you hadn't given up your bachelorhood to live like a monk, and if that's what I thought marriage was all about, I was mistaken. You told me to grow up and learn to stand on my own two feet. And then you left—went stamping off without so much as a goodbye."

"That's more or less it, yes."

"I walked the floor all night after you'd gone, knowing you were right. If your mother bullied me, it was my fault for letting her get away with it, and up to me to put an end to it. But by running away from you?" She shook her head incredulously. "I was running to you. *To you,* Dario Costanzo, because I decided to be the wife you deserved, instead of sniveling in the corner like a whipped puppy."

"Then where did Gauthier fit into the picture?"

"He didn't. His only sin was coming by the next day to tell me he had to return home for health reasons. He had a heart condition that flared up again unexpectedly. I recall thinking he didn't look well and that it was a good thing he was going back to get treatment, but that's about the extent of it because my concern was mainly with you and our marriage. He had to drop off his rental car at the airport, and offered to give me a lift. He might have been en route to Canada via Rome, but I was headed straight to you in Milan."

"And that's all there was to it?"

"In a nutshell. But since you seem to have so little trust in me or my judgment, why don't you ask Yves yourself?"

"I can't. He died in the accident. In fact," Dario said bluntly, "he caused it, though not through any fault of his own. Apparently, he had a heart attack while he was at the wheel."

She pressed her fingers to her mouth, assailed by one shock too many. "Oh, no! I'm sorry to hear that. I had no idea he was so seriously ill. He was such a gentle person, so kind, and much too young to die."

"I'm sorry to be the bearer of more bad news. And I'm sorry that I doubted your loyalty. I'm your husband. I should have trusted you."

"But you didn't, and maybe the reason is that you were looking for an excuse to be rid of me."

"What the devil are you talking about? I married you, didn't I?"

"Oh, yes," she said, the memory of their early days together rising sharp and clear in her mind. "You put on a very good front, were every bit the dutiful husband, both in public and in the privacy of our bedroom, but a front is all it ever was. You proposed only because, when you found out I was expecting your baby, you felt you had no other choice."

"There's a strong element of truth in that, I admit."

She winced, and wondered why this admission, coming as it had on top of others much worse, should leave her feeling so miserably hollow inside. Hadn't she told herself, their last morning in Tunis, that he was a man of honor who would never shirk his responsibilities? Well, that she could still call herself his wife was living proof she'd been right.

"But let me point out that I didn't know you were pregnant when I went to the trouble of looking you up in Vancouver," he continued. "That I did because I cared about you."

She nodded sadly. "'Cared about' is certainly a nice, inoffensive way of putting it."

"What else do you want me to say?"

"That you were at least a little bit in love with me when you married me, as I was with you."

"I can't," he said, the candor she'd once found so disarming striking a fatal blow. "Love came later."

"Did it? You never once told me so. How do you think it made me feel that all the time I was falling more deeply in love with you, you never once said, 'I love you, Maeve'?"

"I'd have thought it was self-evident. If you remember as much as you say you do, you can't have forgotten the nights we spent making love."

"Sex was never a problem for us, Dario. The last few weeks are proof enough of that."

"It was more than sex."

"Not the night I conceived, it wasn't. You made that abundantly clear the next day."

"I know. And nothing I say now can excuse my actions then. The best I can do is tell you I will regret them for the rest of my life. I treated you appallingly for something that was entirely my fault."

"By seducing me, you mean?"

"Yes."

He looked so haunted, so miserable, that she felt constrained to say, "In all fairness, you didn't exactly drag me off kicking and screaming."

"That doesn't absolve me of what followed. All the signs of your innocence were there, if only I hadn't been too self-absorbed to recognize them. Your timidity, your almost catatonic submission…only much later, after we were married, did I realize that you always react that way when you feel under fire or inadequate."

"Was I very inadequate, that first night?"

"No," he said, his gaze soft and warm. "Your honesty and generosity were beautiful. They were what made you so hard to forget. You were like no other woman I'd ever known. I might not have planned to marry you, *amore mio,* but I can tell you in all truth, that I now consider it to be the best decision I've ever made."

"I want to believe you, Dario, I really do," she sighed. "But I keep coming back to the fact that you couldn't be honest with me. You let me think we were on a second honeymoon, when all the time you harbored suspicions that I was going to leave you and take Sebastiano with me. Although," she added, conscience again prodding her to acknowledge that she'd brought some of that on herself, "I suppose I did give you reason to doubt me."

"Does any of it really matter now?" he said, catching her hand and drawing her to him. "This is no longer about what happened in the past, Maeve. It's about you and me, and where we go from here. Mistakes have been made on both sides. Can we not learn from them, forgive ourselves and each other and start over?"

She felt torn clean down the middle, half of her wanting to hate him for deceiving her so well. And half of her simply wanting him. "I'd like to think so, but the way you cut me out of Sebastiano's life, and hid all evidence that he'd ever been born, and kept everyone else away from me…you treated me as if I'd died!"

"In a way you had, Maeve. You weren't the wife I thought you were. At least, that's how it appeared at first. But I know better now. I *have* known better, more or less from the day you came home again. And this last week…*mio dolce,* it truly has been a perfect second honeymoon."

"Really? Is that why you made sure there was no trace of our son at the penthouse, either?"

"There never was much to start with, and the few things you'd left behind I had put in storage weeks ago."

"What do you mean, *left behind?* Are you suggesting you still believe I was running away with him?"

"No, of course I don't. But he spent only the first few weeks of his life there. When you decided you'd rather stay on the island, you took all his things with you, making it very clear to me that you didn't consider the penthouse was your home. The few items you didn't take—some of his clothes and the bassinet—he outgrew ages ago. But if you'll give us another chance to be a family, I'll make a brand-new nursery for him so that he has his own room no matter which place he calls home."

He tucked a stray wisp of hair behind her ear. "What do you say, my love? Can we pick up the pieces and put them together to make it work for all the right reasons this time?"

"I want to," she admitted. "I think so. But…"

"But what?" he said. "Tell me, *tesoro,* and I'll make it happen."

"What I want most is to be with my baby again. Can you make it morning already?"

"Unfortunately not." He stroked his knuckles along her jaw. "But I can think of a way to make the time pass more quickly."

His touch, his voice, tugged at her heartstrings, disarming her. *Be careful,* the voice of caution warned. *You've been through this many times before, where all he had to do was touch you, and you were putty in his hands. But you're not an innocent anymore. You've learned the hard way that it takes more than great sex to build a marriage.*

But her heart knew better than her head. *It takes forgiveness, too. Love, real love, outweighs anger and disappointment. And you love this man, you know you do. You have found your son again. Happiness is at your fingertips, yours for keeps. All you have to do is reach out and take it. Let yesterday go and celebrate a tomorrow that promises true contentment.*

Sighing, she melted against him. Joy permeated her soul. She felt alive, truly alive, at last. She wanted to feel his lips on hers, his hands on her body.

"Show me how," she said.

CHAPTER THIRTEEN

MAEVE didn't complain about the slow passage of time again. From the outset, there'd been a powerful chemistry between her and Dario, a pulsing awareness that might not have been love on his part, but it had held them together during the rough first weeks of their marriage and it was what held them together now.

Not that she could have resisted him, even if she'd tried. He was too skilled a lover, too utterly, gorgeously seductive. Too everything. Any lingering resentment shriveled to dust in the heat of his kisses. His smile, the slumbrous appreciation in his eyes when he looked at her naked body, made her insides flutter as if a thousand tiny wings were beating to get free.

With no more secrets between them, and all the doubts and fears laid to rest, they had no reason to hold back all that lay in their hearts. Every touch, every glance, every whispered word spoke of a newfound trust, one able to withstand whatever fate might hold in store for them.

They had walked through fire and lived to tell about it. Through it all, sex had been their ally, stoking the furnace of their desire when all else failed to bring them together. This time it took them further. Past raw physical need to a deep, quiet intimacy that welded them together seamlessly, in body and in soul.

"I love you, my beautiful wife," he muttered on a fractured breath, seconds before he lost himself in her clinging heat.

They were the sweetest words on earth, and she'd waited what seemed like a lifetime to hear him utter them. They were worth every tortured second, healing her as nothing offered by men of medicine ever could.

Dawn had traced a silver line across the eastern horizon when exhaustion finally caught up with them. Maeve curled up in Dario's arms and fell into a sleep no longer haunted by shadows. She didn't stir until the aroma of coffee brought her awake again.

Squinting in the shaft of sunlight piercing the room, she found Dario standing by the bed, dressed in casual trousers and a polo shirt, and bearing a tall, steaming latte cup. *"Buon giorno, innamorata,"* he murmured, his voice a caress. "Time to get moving."

She stretched drowsily and yawned. "Already?"

"If you want the early start you spoke of last night, then yes. We're leaving in half an hour. If, on the other hand," he added teasingly, "you want to spend the morning in bed with me, that also can be arranged."

"Don't tempt me," she scolded on another yawn, and reached for the coffee mug. "Give me a few minutes to make myself presentable, although how I'll manage to do so might be difficult since, unlike you, all I have at my disposal is an evening gown much the worse for wear. Thank goodness I have my cape to cover up the mess."

"Don't worry about it. No one will see you. I've ordered a helicopter to pick us up here at the yacht and take us to Linate where the company jet's waiting to fly us straight to Pantelleria."

She took a sip of coffee. "I've changed my mind. I want to go to the penthouse to clean myself up and choose something more appropriate to wear for what I have to do before we leave Milan."

"What happened to the mother so anxious to reunite with her son? Last night all you wanted was to be back with Sebastiano as soon as possible."

"I still do. But I have unfinished business to take care of in the city first." She drew in a deep breath and looked him in the eye. "I've made a decision, Dario. I'm going to see your mother. This warfare between us does nobody any good and has to come to an end."

"But Maeve, *angelo mio…!*" He flung out his hands in a manner so quintessentially Italian that she almost laughed. "Are you sure you're up to such an undertaking?"

"I have to be," she said. "I'm a wife and a mother, not a child. It's past time I faced my insecurities for what they really are—weaknesses that only I can conquer. And the place to start is with your mother."

"If that's what you feel you must do, then I'll come with you."

"No. You've protected me long enough. I need to do this alone."

Talk was cheap when more than eighty miles lay between her and her adversary. Bearding the lioness in her den? Not quite as much.

"Thank you for seeing me, Signora Costanzo," Maeve said,

so vibrantly aware of the other woman's scrutiny that it took a great deal of effort not to squirm. "I realize my visit has come as a surprise."

"Indeed." Celeste Costanzo nodded permission for her to perch on the edge of one of two white velvet sofas in a drawing room so tastefully furnished that it defied description.

How does she do it? Maeve wondered. How does she manage to look so perfect in cashmere and pearls, with no sign of last night's fracas leaving bags under her eyes, as Maeve was sure she had under hers? Does she never have a bad hair day? Never smudge her mascara or get a run in her stocking or break a heel?

Taking a seat opposite, Celeste crossed her elegant ankles, folded her manicured hands in her lap and waited, her finely plucked eyebrows raised in silent question.

She wasn't going to make this easy. But then, why should she? Maeve asked herself. When have I ever made things easy for her?

Shoring up her courage, she plunged in. "First, I should tell you that I've recovered my memory. I remember all the events of the past year, up to and including the accident."

"Then I suppose congratulations are in order."

Ah, me! Could she not sometimes give a little, for a change?

Burying a sigh, Maeve plowed on. "I understand your reservations about me, *signora*. I am, as you've so astutely observed on more than one occasion, a nobody, and Dario is a very rich man."

"What is your point, Maeve?" Celeste inquired, her icy demeanor remaining unmoved. "Are you asking my forgiveness for your shortcomings?"

"No," she said staunchly. "I've done nothing to require

your forgiveness. You have a beautiful grandson because of me, and he, by any measure, makes up for whatever disapproval you might hold for his mother."

"Then exactly why are you here?"

"To set the record straight, once and for all, not about who I am not, but about who I am. I don't pretend to have come from the kind of privileged background Dario enjoyed, nor did I achieve the same level of education. However, I am not unintelligent, and most certainly not ashamed of my upbringing. I know the difference between right and wrong, and I have a deeply ingrained sense of fair play."

"And you're baring your soul to me now because?"

"Because whether or not you choose to believe me, there was no affair between me and Yves Gauthier. We happened both to be Canadian, and that was our only connection. I love Dario. I have from the day I met him, and I always will. We've not had an easy time of it, these last few months, but we *are* a team and I will allow nothing to come between us ever again. Not another man, not a near-death experience…and not you, Signora Costanzo."

"I see. Is that all?"

Was that grudging respect Maeve saw in her eyes? Bolstered by the possibility, she said, "No. If my son one day were to present me with the fait accompli of a pregnant stranger as a daughter-in-law, my initial reaction would be one of deep concern. Words such as *entrapment* and *fortune hunter* and *social climber* might occur to me, as I'm sure they have to you."

"Then we share something in common, after all."

"What we have in common, Signora Costanzo, is that we

both love Dario and we both love Sebastiano. I am not asking you to love me as well, but can we not overlook our differences and, for the sake of our families, forge a closer relationship, one based on mutual respect, if not affection?"

"I don't see that happening," Celeste said.

Her reply, spoken with such uncompromising certainty, reduced Maeve's hard-won courage to a deflated heap.

"At least," Celeste added, a hint of something approaching warmth in her tone, and her mouth almost turning up in a smile, "not if you persist in calling me Signora Costanzo."

She wanted to be called Mother? One day, perhaps, Maeve thought, balking at the idea. But now was too much, too soon.

"*'Madre'* would be a little premature, of course," Celeste continued with unnerving prescience, "but do you suppose you could bring yourself to call me Celeste?"

Maeve had been gone more than two hours, during which time Dario paced the floor like the anxious expectant father of triplets. He never should have allowed her to confront Celeste alone. He loved his mother, but he was under no illusions about her ability to reduce the most assured individual to babbling idiocy, if she so chose. And although Maeve was certainly no idiot, underneath her smart navy blue jacket and skirt, she was a fragile, vulnerable woman.

When she did finally show up at the penthouse, all she'd say was that she'd bring him up to speed later, but that her most immediate concern now was to get to the airport and head home to Sebastiano. Since he was equally anxious to reunite with their son, he called for the car to be brought round.

She settled in the backseat, a Mona Lisa smile on her face,

and smoothed her skirt over her long legs. Grinding his teeth, he did his best to curb his trademark impatience. But when, some ten minutes later, they'd left the toll zone and were traveling along the Via Marco Bruto, no more than a couple of kilometers from the airport, he could contain himself no longer.

"You're going to keep me hanging until the last possible minute, aren't you?"

"Yes," she replied saucily. "It's my turn to be the one with all the answers."

"At least tell me it wasn't horrible."

She patted his hand reassuringly. "Do you see blood?"

"No, but nor did I expect to. My mother doesn't need a knife to inflict wounds. She can slice a person open with one look."

"Oh, I learned many years ago to withstand that kind of attack, Dario. You ought to know that by now."

"I'm beginning to think I don't know the half of it. When did my shy, defenseless wife turn into such a warrior?"

She leaned closer and kissed his cheek. "When her husband told her he loved her."

"How could I not?" he muttered, embarrassed to find his throat thick with sudden emotion. "You overwhelm me, my lovely Maeve. I know of no one with a bigger heart, and I thank God that you gave it to me, even if I was at first too blind to recognize how lucky I am."

"It isn't how you start out, it's where you end up," she said sagely. "We're together, and will soon have our son again. For me that means everything. Tell me about him, Dario. What's he like now? Have his eyes changed color? Does he still have lots of hair?"

"He's grown, as you'd expect, has two bottom teeth, one

top, and is almost crawling. But his eyes are as blue as yours, and his hair as dark and curly as ever."

"I can't wait to see him," she said wistfully. "Do you think he'll recognize me?"

The car swung into the airport and drew up near the tarmac where the jet waited. "You'll soon find out, *amore*," he said. "We'll be back on the island in a little more than three hours—just enough time to enjoy a leisurely in-flight lunch with Giuliana and Lorenzo, who are also headed home today."

When he stepped into the main cabin, however, he discovered his parents were onboard, as well. "This is unexpected," he remarked, noting the open bottle of champagne and general air of festivity. "I was under the impression you were staying in Milan for the next few days."

His mother nodded. "We were, but plans changed at the last minute."

He swung his gaze to Maeve, who appeared not the least taken aback by their presence. "You don't seem surprised," he said.

"I'm not," she informed him airily. "I invited your parents to join us when I visited Celeste this morning."

Celeste? Invited?

"Uh-huh," he grunted. "Anything else I should know about?"

Giuliana snickered into her champagne. No great surprise there. She'd always been a giggler. It used to drive him crazy when they were young.

"A little dinner party for six tonight," Maeve warbled. "I phoned Antonia from your mom's this morning to arrange it. It seemed only right that the whole family should be there to celebrate the grand reunion."

"A glass of champagne, son?" his father asked.

"I need something stronger, *Babbo*," he said. "Make it a Scotch, instead."

Almost midnight, with a light breeze lifting the filmy drapes at the open bedroom doors behind her, and the slate tiles beneath her bare feet still warm from the afternoon sun. Across the sea, lights twinkled on the Tunisian coast. The end of a glorious, momentous day, Maeve thought, breathing deeply of the sweetly scented air.

So many memories. Celeste smiling conspiratorially at her across the aircraft cabin. Dario's face, priceless in its astonishment. "People don't effect a coup like this and get away with it," he'd threatened her in an undertone, when they sat down for lunch. "You're safe enough now, but you'll pay for this later, once we're alone."

Arriving at the villa, to find the entire household staff waiting on the front steps to welcome her home. Flowers in every room. Her little niece, Cristina, adorable in white embroidered cotton and lace, planting a shy kiss on her cheek and calling her Zia Maeve. Enrica, the cook, taking her aside to consult on the dinner menu. "Does it meet with your approval, Signora Costanzo?"

Dario disappearing briefly, then returning with their son and placing him in her arms. To hold him again, to smell his sweet, clean baby smell, feel his breath against her neck, his chubby fingers clutching her hair, the warmth of his little body against hers, his wide smile not quite as gummy anymore...that was a heaven on earth made all the more unforgettable by the emotional response of those who witnessed it. Lorenzo and Edmondo blinking furiously. Giuliana sobbing openly. Celeste dabbing fastidiously at her eyes with a scrap of lace that passed for a handkerchief. And Dario whispering, "Look, *angelo mio,* he remembers you. Sebastiano knows his mother."

With a last glance at the star-studded night, Maeve turned and went on silent feet through the bedroom to the nursery. A lamp on the dresser sent out a soft glow, enough to show a yellow plush teddy bear sitting in the rocking chair near the window. She crossed to the crib and looked at her sleeping son. He lay on his back with his arms outflung.

"Perfect, isn't he?" Dario whispered, coming up behind her and slipping his arm around her waist.

"Perfect," she echoed, and pressing a kiss to her fingertip, she placed it gently on her baby's rosy cheek. "I love him so much."

Dario turned her away. "And I love you. Come to bed now, my darling, and let me show you how much."

She went with him, his words alone enough to unfurl the passion always lurking in her soul. She was home at last. The two people who meant the most to her were under this one roof.

They loved her.

She loved them.

It was enough. It was everything.

Joy spilled over her, rich and warm and forever.

* * * * *

Kay Young returned to woozy consciousness to find that she was lying on a soft sofa beneath a heap of quilts near a cheerfully burning fire. When she tried to move, however, everything hurt, and she groaned.

At once she heard a sound, then a stranger with a hard, harsh face was squatting beside her. "Shh," he said softly. "You're safe here. I promise."

"I have to go," she said weakly, struggling against pain. "He'll find me. He can't find me."

"Easy, lady," he said quietly. "You're hurt. No one's going to find you here."

"He will," she said desperately, terror clutching at her insides. "He always finds me!"

"Easy," he said again. "There's a blizzard outside. No one's getting here tonight, not even the doctor. I know, because I tried."

"Doctor? I don't need a doctor! I've got to get away."

"There's nowhere to go tonight," he said levelly. "And if I thought you could stand, I'd take you to a window and show you."

But even as she tried once more to pull away the quilts, she remembered something else: this man had been gentle when he'd found her beside the road, even when she had kicked and clawed. He hadn't hurt her.

Terror receded just a bit. She looked at him and detected signs of true concern there.

The terror eased another notch and she let her head sag on the pillow. "He always finds me," she whispered.

"Not here. Not tonight. That much I can guarantee."

Will Kay's mysterious rescuer protect her
from her worst fears?
Find out in HER HERO IN HIDING by New York Times
bestselling author Rachel Lee.
Available June 2010, only from
Silhouette® Romantic Suspense.

HARLEQUIN® *Romance*®

GIRLS' Weekend in VEGAS

Four friends, four dream weddings!

On a girly weekend in Las Vegas, best friends Alex, Molly,
Serena and Jayne are supposed to just have fun and forget
men, but they end up meeting their perfect matches!
Will the love they find in Vegas stay in Vegas?

Find out in this sassy, fun and wildly romantic miniseries
all about love and friendship!

Saving Cinderella! by MYRNA MACKENZIE
Available June

Vegas Pregnancy Surprise by SHIRLEY JUMP
Available July

Inconveniently Wed! by JACKIE BRAUN
Available August

Wedding Date with the Best Man
by MELISSA McCLONE
Available September

www.eHarlequin.com

HR17663

LARGER-PRINT BOOKS!

HARLEQUIN *Presents*

PASSION GUARANTEED SEDUCTION

GET 2 FREE LARGER-PRINT NOVELS PLUS 2 FREE GIFTS!

YES! Please send me 2 FREE LARGER-PRINT Harlequin Presents® novels and my 2 FREE gifts (gifts are worth about $10). After receiving them, if I don't wish to receive any more books, I can return the shipping statement marked "cancel". If I don't cancel, I will receive 6 brand-new novels every month and be billed just $4.55 per book in the U.S. or $5.24 per book in Canada. That's a saving of at least 13% off the cover price! It's quite a bargain! Shipping and handling is just 50¢ per book.* I understand that accepting the 2 free books and gifts places me under no obligation to buy anything. I can always return a shipment and cancel at any time. Even if I never buy another book, the two free books and gifts are mine to keep forever.

176/376 HDN E5NG

Name _____ (PLEASE PRINT) _____

Address _____ Apt. # _____

City _____ State/Prov. _____ Zip/Postal Code _____

Signature (if under 18, a parent or guardian must sign) _____

Mail to the **Harlequin Reader Service:**
IN U.S.A.: P.O. Box 1867, Buffalo, NY 14240-1867
IN CANADA: P.O. Box 609, Fort Erie, Ontario L2A 5X3

Not valid for current subscribers to Harlequin Presents Larger-Print books.

**Are you a subscriber to Harlequin Presents books
and want to receive the larger-print edition?
Call 1-800-873-8635 today!**

* Terms and prices subject to change without notice. Prices do not include applicable taxes. Sales tax applicable in N.Y. Canadian residents will be charged applicable provincial taxes and GST. Offer not valid in Quebec. This offer is limited to one order per household. All orders subject to approval. Credit or debit balances in a customer's account(s) may be offset by any other outstanding balance owed by or to the customer. Please allow 4 to 6 weeks for delivery. Offer available while quantities last.

Your Privacy: Harlequin Books is committed to protecting your privacy. Our Privacy Policy is available online at www.eHarlequin.com or upon request from the Reader Service. From time to time we make our lists of customers available to reputable third parties who may have a product or service of interest to you. If you would prefer we not share your name and address, please check here. ☐

Help us get it right—We strive for accurate, respectful and relevant communications. To clarify or modify your communication preferences, visit us at www.ReaderService.com/consumerschoice.

HPLP10R